Nineteen Seventy-Five

THE SEVEN BOOK FIVE

SARAH M. CRADIT

Cover Design by Sarah M. Cradit
Editing by Lawrence Editing

ISBN: 978-1-958744-28-4

Publisher Contact:
sarah@sarahmcradit.com
www.sarahmcradit.com

Preface

If you're here, you've hopefully started with *1970,* followed by *1972, 1973,* and *1974*.

This is the fifth book of seven, and if you're a reader of *The House of Crimson & Clover,* you might begin to see the future come together quite neatly—and, in some cases, tragically—in this story. When I wrote *The House of Crimson & Clover* and the accompanying histories of the characters you're reading about now, many years before *The Seven* was even planned, I remember 1975 as being a watershed year for the Deschanels, in more ways than one. I made that decision long before I ever decided to write this series, and it's a decision that shaped every character involved, past and future.

There are benefits to knowing the general histories before sitting down to write an origin series. To have the high-level timeline already mapped out makes outlining that much easier, and I've surprised myself with how well the past and future flow together. But the downside is that what is written in canon cannot be changed. And while my past self, writing for the future, decided 1975 would be a significant year for the family, my present self, writing for the past, felt the emotional toll of that decision.

1975 is a story filled with equal amounts of joy and tragedy. It's a banner year, one that sets up both the remainder of this series and

The House of Crimson & Clover, where the children of *The Seven* are the lead characters. This book will likely be an emotional roller-coaster to read, just as it was to write, but—and if you tell the other books this, I'll deny it—for these reasons and more, it's my favorite in the series so far. Knowing what I know now, I wouldn't go back and change a thing about the year 1975. As we know, in real life, big years happen. We can all look back on certain years of our life as being a little bit *more.*

One thing I feel compelled to point out, as I believe I have in prior books: Although I mention *The House of Crimson & Clover* several times, it's not necessary to read that series to fully appreciate *The Seven.* I do, however, hope that when this series ends, it leaves you feeling the urge to see what happens next, for both these characters and their children. The Saga of Crimson & Clover is designed to have multiple ways of experiencing the world that never need to connect, unless you want them to, but I'll always hope I've done my job by making you want them to.

As with the earlier novels in the series, I feel it's important to add the disclaimer that I was not alive at any point in the '70s. I was raised on the music, values, and results of that period, coming up in the '80s with a vision of the world that matched what my parents had experienced in that pivotal decade. I've leveraged experiences and memories of those who did come of age in the era, but any errors are solely my own. If this paragraph looks familiar, you probably read a version of it in the Prefaces of the earlier books.

Lastly, if you've read the short story *A Band of Heather,* you'll recognize a story involving Colleen (no spoilers) that is also told here, in *1975.* The short was written years before this series was planned, so to remain true to both, some of the passages are very similar, though this book expands considerably upon that original story. *A Band of Heather* was meant to be a glimpse into that piece of Colleen's life, whereas this is a full look.

With all that said, proceed with a full heart and an open mind. Tissues wouldn't hurt, either.

Also by Sarah M. Cradit

KINGDOM OF THE WHITE SEA

Kingdom of the White Sea Trilogy

The Kingless Crown

The Broken Realm

The Hidden Kingdom

The Book of All Things

Blackwood Cycle

The Raven and the Rush

The Poison and the Paladin

Southerlands Cycle

The Sylvan and the Sand

The Flame and the Forsaken

Guardians Cycle

The Altruist and the Assassin

The Belle and the Blackbird

Darkwood Cycle

The Melody and the Master

The Hand and the Heart

Sceptre Cycle

The Claw and the Crowned

The Duke and the Disciple

THE SAGA OF CRIMSON & CLOVER

The House of Crimson and Clover Series

The Storm and the Darkness

Shattered

The Illusions of Eventide

Bound

Midnight Dynasty

Asunder

Empire of Shadows

Myths of Midwinter

The Hinterland Veil

The Secrets Amongst the Cypress

Within the Garden of Twilight

House of Dusk, House of Dawn

Midnight Dynasty Series

A Tempest of Discovery

A Storm of Revelations

A Torrent of Deceit

The Seven Series

Nineteen Seventy

Nineteen Seventy-Two

Nineteen Seventy-Three

Nineteen Seventy-Four

Nineteen Seventy-Five

Nineteen Seventy-Six

Nineteen Eighty

Vampires of the Merovingi Series

The Island

and more

The Dusk Trilogy

St. Charles at Dusk: The Story of Oz and Adrienne

Flourish: The Story of Anne Fontaine

Banshee: The Story of Giselle Deschanel

Crimson & Clover Stories

Available as a single collection, The Shorts

Surrender: The Story of Oz and Ana

Shame: The Story of Jonathan St. Andrews

Fire & Ice: The Story of Remy & Fleur

Dark Blessing: The Landry Triplets

Pandora's Box: The Story of Jasper & Pandora

The Menagerie: Oriana's Den of Iniquities

A Band of Heather: The Story of Colleen and Noah

The Ephemeral: The Story of Autumn & Gabriel

Bayou's Edge: The Landry Triplets

For more information, and exciting bonus material, visit www. sarahmcradit.com

The Seven in 1975

Children of
August Deschanel (deceased) &
Colleen "Irish Colleen" Brady

Charles August Deschanel, Aged 25
Augustus Charles Deschanel, Aged 24
Colleen Amelia Deschanel, Aged 23
Madeline Colleen Deschanel, Deceased
Evangeline Julianne Deschanel, Aged 21
Maureen Amelia Deschanel, Aged 19
Elizabeth Jeanne Deschanel, Aged 16

For Colleen

SPRING 1975

NEW ORLEANS, LOUISIANA
VACHERIE, LOUISIANA
CAMBRIDGE, MASSACHUSETTS
EDINBURGH, SCOTLAND

Prologue: Irish Colleen and the Seven

Colleen Deschanel, known as Irish Colleen to her family and friends, walked past the faces of her seven children, as she did every night of her life.

Charles' icy eyes penetrated from his senior picture. She had better pictures of him... less overtly hostile, ones betraying a softer side to her hardened son. She should replace this with one of those, but as she thought of him living his loveless life, in his hollow ancestral home, she didn't deserve his smile. The brutal intensity of his gaze reminded her of her role in his unhappiness. One hand of her penance.

Augustus' picture was no better. If Charles was fueled by his rage, Augustus bottled his sadness and turned it into steeled determination. His drawn look belied his stoic resolve, his absolute commitment to anything in life that brought results without expending too much emotion. His marriage to the sullen Ekatherina had thrown a wrench into his life that had the potential to break him far more than Madeline had.

Irish Colleen didn't know which of her sons she worried for more.

Her oldest daughter, her namesake, Colleen, beamed a dutiful, if impatient smile from her spot on the mantle. Taking a picture, like so many things, was a waste of time for Colleen, who was always looking for what was next, what higher bar she could reach for. She'd reached across the ocean this time, and Scotland seemed to brighten her in a way nothing at home ever had. Irish Colleen suspected, even, that Colleen had met someone, though she held out no hope of news, for Colleen was deeply private.

At least she would be home this summer. Nearly a year had passed since she'd last seen her, and Irish Colleen could tell no one of how much her absence hurt, for this pain was necessary for her daughter to spread her wings and grow.

As for Madeline, the next face on her nightly journey, there would be no wings. Irish Colleen said a prayer for her daughter's soul and moved on.

Evangeline was gone now, maybe forever. Even when she was a baby, Irish Colleen looked upon her fifth child with a sense she was peering upon someone who was not one of them. It was a terrible thing to think about one's own child, and Irish Colleen spent many, many nights praying for the feeling to go away. But when it did not, she learned, instead, to embrace the "otherness" of Evangeline and push her toward the greatness she was born for. Irish Colleen lacked the education or the resourcefulness to know where Evangeline's life should take her, but she knew enough to keep pushing. Always pushing. She didn't know if Evangeline would ever come home. If she didn't, it might not be the worst thing.

Irish Colleen prayed over that feeling, too.

And Maureen... Maureen, her child, through and through. Maureen didn't know this, and never would, because Irish Colleen preferred the way her children saw her, even if it wasn't the entire picture. Irish Colleen was seventeen when she fell pregnant with Charles, and she wasn't the unwitting pawn others saw her to be. Nor had August Deschanel been her first.

Maureen wasn't speaking to her now, but she would. When Maureen was a mother, she would finally understand what it meant to sacrifice, and in doing so, give up the foolish dream of deeper happiness. The matter of her marriage to the Blanchard had been, for once, not Irish Colleen's doing, though she didn't disagree with it, either. Maureen could do so much worse, and almost had.

Irish Colleen climbed the stairs and made her way toward Elizabeth's room. Elizabeth was sixteen now, and there was nothing, not in the way her sinewy limbs had turned to curves, nor in the intensity of her knowing gaze, that allowed for a glimpse into the girl she'd only very recently been. Something else had changed Lizzy, something Irish Colleen wasn't privy to, for once.

She was afraid of her youngest daughter. She always had been, truth be told, but to see Elizabeth become a woman made her danger all the more real. Elizabeth held within her dark truths that had been slowly destroying her, and the shell required to live with such darkness did not come without a price.

Elizabeth wasn't sleeping. She wasn't even in her room. She hovered at the end of the hall, not in a nightgown anymore, but in a pair of cotton briefs and a tank top. She leaned over the desk just under the dormer window, which had been a selling point of the house. Elizabeth had loved the dormer window in their house near the cemetery, and there was very little Elizabeth loved. Irish Colleen had so few opportunities to do something meaningful for her.

"What're you looking at?"

"The rain," Elizabeth said. She wrapped her ankles together and leaned further forward. "Probably our last storm of the season that won't feel like a sauna."

"You'll freeze in that," Irish Colleen admonished. She unwrapped her own shawl and moved to drape it over Elizabeth.

"Stop," Elizabeth said, shrugging it away. "You have the heat jacked up to eighty. I can hardly breathe."

"Well, I'll turn it down then," Irish Colleen said, slighted. "Goodness, you've never complained before."

"What would be the point?"

"Don't get sassy with me, missy."

"What do you want me to say, Mama? Shit, you've never liked anyone questioning you."

"Elizabeth! That mouth!"

"I guess I should get the soap?"

Irish Colleen spun her daughter around. Elizabeth fell back on the balls of her feet, glowering. "What has gotten into you?" She touched the back of her hand to her forehead. "You don't feel warm."

"Lord in heaven, as if every time I'm cranky it must mean I'm with fever!"

"Elizabeth!"

"Well, Mama, ask me already! That's why you're here, isn't it? To get your semi-annual premonition, designed to make me feel even more helpless as I watch you brood through your guessing games?"

"You really are *not* yourself, Lizzy. I might just call your doctor..."

"You call him and I won't be here." Elizabeth crossed her arms. Her eyes glowed in the dark hall, set to the dark tones of the storm outside. She was the storm inside. "I'm tired. Tired of everything. You wanna know what's happening to our family this year, Mama? Births! Deaths! Two for one special!" She threw her hands up in the air. "There? You happy now?"

Elizabeth stormed into her room and slammed the door.

CHAPTER 1

A Lovely Secret

Colleen watched the sun slowly rise over Edinburgh, as the light made its slow approach over the room, cutting a bright swash across the patchwork comforter. She rested her left hand in the thick band of sunlight and turned it to and fro, admiring the heartiness of her dried heather band.

Beside her, Noah slept.

In the end is our beginning, he'd said, and oh, how much had changed in the span of only a few days, set to the magic of Skye.

AFTER THAT AFTERNOON AT THE FAIRY POOL, THEY'D spent the following days of their lovers' respite traveling the windy roads of Skye, hiking the jagged cliffs of Storr, enjoying porridge at a small inn in Uig, and traversing the Fairy Glen, which resonated with even more magic than the pools. Colleen had fallen in love with the sloping, hilly glen, and the fairy circles, insisting, to Noah's amusement, on leaving an offering for the mysterious beings.

"You believe in this, do you, my goddess of science?"

"I believe in everything, even those things science can't explain."

Noah kissed her and left his own offering, to please her.

They'd navigated the island like intrepid explorers, never tiring of discovery, or each other. Their evenings they spent wrapped in embrace, sharing every corner of their souls, except the darkest.

What will become of us when we return to the world? she had thought then, and still, now, didn't have the answer.

On New Year's Eve, as their trip neared its end, she'd beseeched Noah to take her back to the magical glen. She had one last wish of the fairies.

As she'd traced her path into the circle of stones—first forward, then, after making her offering and speaking her wish—retracing them backward through the spiral, Noah discovered his own bit of magic: a patch of purple heather, untouched by the changing of the seasons.

He found Colleen gazing up at the summit of Castle Ewan. "Colleen." His voice cracked.

She turned to see him holding a small circle of woven heather. "Whatever lives we both left behind in New Orleans, they'll always be a part of us, but we're different people now. We both want to matter. I say, we can matter together. I say, in the end is *our* beginning, Colleen."

Noah held the small band of heather toward her. Colleen saw, in the light of his words, what it truly was: a ring. "You're proposing?" she'd whispered.

The corner of his mouth cracked into a grin. "Only if you're accepting."

We hardly know each other, she knew she should say. The voice of a reasonable woman, a woman of science and logic, as she counted herself. But she did know him. They'd exchanged a hundred silent words between them for every one spoken aloud, and she'd fallen in love with him without realizing the moment of inception.

"I'm accepting," Colleen replied, releasing a sound that was half-crying, half-laughter. Who was this carefree woman, stepping into a future with both eyes closed and her heart wide-open? Who had she become?

"Christmas," he managed to say between kisses. "We can do it next year, or we can do it ten years from now, but I want to marry you on Christmas."

"Our day, from now on. Always," she agreed.

Christmas.

Christmas Eve, though, would always be Maddy's.

WINTER FADED TO SPRING. SHE SHARED HERSELF, IN every way, except one. Every way, except the most important, the most fundamental, for a Deschanel.

He didn't know she was a witch, and she feared what he'd do with that knowledge, given his own family's history. His entire family had fallen apart because of his mother's apparent involvement in witchcraft, and Noah hadn't seen her, or his three sisters, since he was young, too young to have any memories.

She eventually wrote to Evangeline and told her the whole, sordid, wonderful story. Evangeline's advice? *Jump in with both feet and learn to swim together.*

Easy for Evangeline to say, when she didn't have her heart dangling over a cliff.

Colleen brushed her lips against Noah's forehead and went to make coffee. As she assembled the tasks needed, her thoughts drifted to home. Almost a year into her residency in Scotland, she felt the first pang of being needed back in New Orleans. She didn't know where it was coming from, though it wouldn't surprise her if her own big life changes were at the root of this strange feeling of uncertainty. Noah asked, gently but at least once a week, when they could share the good news with their families, and she insisted it was better said in person.

She believed this, but there was more to it, more she was afraid to say, even to Noah, whom she'd let crawl around inside her soul and take a peek at spots in the corners once reserved only for her. She'd opened the protective compartments and let him in, and it wasn't as bad as she thought... to the contrary, it was refreshing to not have the need to hide in solitude. Noah let the light in.

Her fear was founded in the belief that her family saw her as the sane one. The unfailing pragmatist who carefully calculated every decision, even the small ones, but *especially* the big ones. What would they think of her, to learn she'd spent a week with a man she hardly knew and, at the end of it, accepted his proposal of marriage? More, that she was now months into this engagement and having no regrets over such a foolish, errant moment of weakness?

Colleen was not ashamed to be marrying Noah Jameson, not even a little. His position in society back home might make her mother cringe, but Colleen was a third child of August Deschanel, not the heir, or even the spare. Marrying beneath her station was an antiquated notion, in any case, one Colleen had no time for. She'd love him just as much if he were homeless, or if he were a millionaire, because she'd fallen for the man, not the place setting.

But what would they all *think*? She was supposed to be the rational one! The level head!

Let's go when the spring term is over, Colleen. Go see both our families, tell them our wonderful news. It would be wrong to keep all this happiness to ourselves. Downright selfish, even.

Colleen found Noah's enthusiasm contagious. So contagious that every time he talked about their future, she couldn't help leading him to the bedroom. Love was sexy. Commitment was sexy. *He* was sexy. And he was hers.

She'd need to get in front of her family before they said something foolish. They'd probably assume she'd already told Noah who she was and what she could do, and though she hadn't yet figured out how to tell him any of it, she knew unequivocally it must come from her.

End of spring. It wasn't so far away, but everything would be different. She'd be an aunt for the first time. Maureen's child was due any day, and Charles' son would be coming only weeks after. Evangeline wouldn't be there, because she'd opted to stay in Massachusetts for the summer. And Colleen would be engaged to the man of her dreams.

She sighed and poured a steaming hot cup of coffee.

Noah's arms slid around her from behind. "Smells like chicory. *Please* tell me you found some chicory here."

"Maybe," she teased.

"There's nothing from home I miss more."

"Not even your dad?" She spun in his arms so she could see his face. She never tired of it. Could spend hours studying each curve, each line; running her hands over his light stubble decorating a strong jaw.

"Sorry, Dad, chicory wins." Noah reached behind her to take a sip of her coffee. He feigned pouring the cup over her head and she winced and giggled. *Giggled.* When had Colleen, ever, in her life, giggled?

"I was thinking we should buy the plane tickets today." Colleen nuzzled herself into his chest, still warm from sleep.

"Only if you stop trying to pay for mine."

Colleen pulled herself back. Kissed him, letting her lips linger another moment. "We've talked about this. The money is nothing to me. It's everything to you. Let me do this for you."

"Wanna take the silver spoon out of your mouth and try again?"

Colleen playfully socked him.

"I'm going to be your husband, Colleen," Noah said. "I have to be able to care for you."

"That's a very old-fashioned notion of marriage," she said lightly. "And if you're hoping to compete with my inheritance, you'll always be disappointed. I didn't have any say into what I was born with. And besides, you *will* be a force of your own when you're a doctor. We won't need my money."

Noah frowned. "It's easy to act like money doesn't matter when you've always had more than you could ever need."

Colleen kissed him again. "You're right. I'm sorry. But it *is* more than I could ever need, so why not let me share it with you? Save your money for our new place."

"Our new place." Noah's smile returned. "I can't wait to live with you. I always forget my damn toothbrush here, and I never have clean underwear at home."

"That's because you never do any laundry," she chided. "But, of course, you're the one who will care for me, right?"

"I oughta wash your mouth out," Noah hissed and lifted her to the counter. He parted her robe with his hips as he moved in on her. His hands slid up her inner thigh, eyes widening when he realized she wasn't wearing underwear. His groin throbbed against her, through his pajama pants.

"With what?" Colleen purred and then abruptly gasped as he entered her and silenced her with several delicious, sharp thrusts.

NOAH SNORED SOFTLY, ASLEEP ONCE MORE. COLLEEN peeled herself from the bed with great reluctance. She only had a short window before he'd be awake, and then they'd be focused on their studying, as they did every Sunday afternoon.

Colleen slipped into the small office on the second floor and picked up the phone. She hesitated before dialing. She'd been a terrible niece. In her attempt to let her family govern themselves, Ophelia became collateral damage. For Colleen, it was all or nothing, and that left her relationship with her great-aunt hanging in the balance.

Ophelia answered on the first ring. "I expected this call five minutes ago."

"You know me, Tante." Colleen swallowed. "How are you?"

Ophelia's gravelly cough filled the line. "If you're winding up for some sort of apology for looking after yourself, spare us both, Colleen. I'm due for a nap."

"Oh, I'm sorry, should I call—"

"Stop it. We both know you need advice, and we both know what about."

Colleen laughed. "Why do I even bother?"

"I won't tell you your future," Ophelia said. "You turned me down once for divination, and I believe that was your truest self who rejected that offer. I won't have you blaming me for coercing you into a glimpse."

"I wouldn't do that."

"No, because I'm not going to tell you your future, now am I?"

"Tante..."

"Here's your advice. Are you listening? I'm quite tired."

"Yes, ma'am." Colleen sighed. It was so good to hear her aunt's voice. That old comfort of knowing you were talking with one of the ancients. One of the good ones. The ones who knew.

"Overthinking breeds fear. Your fears have always come from your inability to stop ruining the good things in your life with analyzing them into the ground. Stop doing that. Just stop it."

"It's so hard when my brain's natural state is to consider all possible outcomes."

Ophelia coughed again. She sounded so old now. So much had changed in just a year. Colleen's heart ached. "It's okay to think with your heart sometimes, Colleen. Men will tell you your heart is weak and can't be trusted, but your heart speaks the loudest and the clearest, if you stop and listen. Our heart gives us the courage our mind would refuse us. Our heart gives those around us something special to carry with them when we're gone. Our heart is an extension of our soul. Yes, your mind is a beautiful thing, and you were gifted with an especially good one. But it is not your mind, Colleen, that will warm you in the coldest nights. It is not your mind that will hold your hand when you need comfort. Your heart is who you are, and to push it aside, to... to deny it what it most wants is to deny yourself a chance at real happiness."

Colleen wiped the tears from her eyes and worked to compose herself for a response, but the line was dead.

COLIN AND CATHERINE'S BABY SHOWER ENDED UP occurring *after* the birth of their first son, Colin Austin Sullivan III, who made his grand entrance three weeks ahead of schedule. Named Colin, for his father, and Austin, for Catherine's father, by the end of the first week of his life they decided two Colins in the same house was one too many, and so they called him Austin.

That wasn't quite right either, though. He didn't look like an Austin, with his jet-black hair and beaming eyes that Colin insisted would end up green like his and his father's, Sullivan through and through. One of the Sullivan cousins who flowed in and out to greet the newest heir finally settled the matter, entirely by accident.

"Aussy... Aussty... Ozzy..." he stammered.

The young couple exchanged a look. Catherine said, "Ahh, Ozzy! There it is!" And Colin said, "How about just Oz?"

And so Oz was the second born child to the Sullivan clan in the generation, after Clancy, though being the son of Colin II and grandson of Colin I, and so on, drawing a straight line down from all the esteemed Sullivan men who had built their empire, ensured he would be first in everything in life. Especially where the law firm was concerned.

Rory and Carolina had flown back for the baby shower, but instead walked into a new nephew to love. Carolina's dark-lidded eyes and sallow cheeks were hard to look upon, and Charles had half a mind to put Colleen on the job. But he'd heard a rumor that Colleen had already visited Carolina Sullivan once, and that this visit might be why Carolina survived the ordeal at all.

Cordelia attended the shower with Charles, looking ready to burst as well. She had eight weeks left, though she said the women in her family always delivered early, declaring this as a statement of scientific fact. Pregnancy tamed his wife in a way nothing else so far had. Her remarks were less cutting, and she was even agreeable from time to time. She no longer pitched a fit when he wanted to come with her to the doctor's appointments, which had increased in frequency as of late, and tolerated spending a couple minutes after with him discussing what they'd learned. She'd even moved back into Ophélie, when he insisted she needed a full staff—and husband—attending her in these final days.

Charles wouldn't go as far as to say he liked his wife, but life had settled some, and for that, he was grateful.

"Congrats, my man," Charles said, one hand clapped to Colin's back, the other peeling back the light blue blanket covering Oz's sweet face. "Like all Sullivans, he showed up early and made everyone else look bad."

Colin laughed. "I'm glad he's here, but I wish he'd shown up on time instead. We weren't quite ready for his arrival."

Charles leveled a skeptical gaze. "A Sullivan? Not ready?"

"Thank goodness for Catherine. She's such a natural. She was meant for this." They watched, together, as a glowing Catherine showed her new son off to a group of doting women.

Yes, thought Charles. *She was meant for this, but it doesn't make me ready to see it.*

The contrast between the woman he married and the woman he loved was like standing in the storm and watching the sun off in the distance. Cordelia pretended to be interested in the Sullivan baby, but she played the part expected of her. Said all the right things and inserted the appropriate dosage of "oohs" and "oh dears" as Catherine proudly told of how her baby launched his breakfast all over her new dress, or how she learned the hard way how to properly change a baby boy's diaper.

Catherine's radiance was soul-deep. She *was* meant for this, the nurturing of another. Whatever peace she'd made or not made with her marriage, it had all come down to this moment. She was the warm, glowing center of the room, and everyone, everything else, paled next to the force of her love.

Colin rejoined his wife, and Cordelia appeared at Charles' side. "Be fortunate that baby has black hair, Charles," she said, with a mischievous twinkle.

Was she goading him? Being playful? He wouldn't know how to recognize it if she was. "I'll pretend I don't know what you mean."

"You're quite good at that. Pretending."

"And you, my dear, are getting better." He tipped his glass of cognac at her.

"I don't want a baby shower," she declared suddenly. "I know I'm the one who said I did, but this child is taking all my energy, and I'm weary of parties, in any case. And do we really need others to spend money on us? Seems trite and in poor form."

Charles could almost appreciate her practicality. "It's your decision. If you don't want a shower, we'll cancel."

"You're upset with me."

Charles laughed. "Upset? Do you think I want to be at *this* baby shower, let alone one where I have to be gracious and talk to everyone?"

"Yes, darling, but you don't want to be at *this* baby shower because of *her.*" Cordelia had the good sense not to point, but she didn't need to.

"It's over. Past," Charles insisted, more for himself. If he said it enough, he might one day believe it. "Their child puts a seal on it."

"Their child," Cordelia repeated. She wrapped both arms over the top of her protruding belly. "Too bad Catherine has no one to remind her to practice good sense and stop looking over at you every chance she gets."

"I wish she wouldn't," Charles murmured into his glass. "I don't know what else to say to make her move on."

"Here's a compliment, Charles," Cordelia said. "I appreciate your restraint where she's concerned. I know that's difficult for you, and I didn't make it any easier with that party I threw months ago. But *someone* has to get her to sing from the same hymnal, or that child that looks like every other Sullivan brooding around New Orleans won't be enough to save her. And if she goes down? I fear you, and this family, go with her."

Cordelia went home early, complaining of fatigue, accepting a ride from Irish Colleen. Charles stayed long past most of the guests without realizing, until he looked around and there was only Colin and Catherine.

"I better head out myself," he said.

"Actually," Colin said. He stood and gave his crisp suit a quick tug. "I need to head to the office for an hour or so."

"Colin! Today, even?" Catherine exclaimed.

"Unfortunately, but Charles is here and... Charles, you don't mind sitting with Cat and Oz for a bit, do you?"

Catherine's and Charles' eyes widened in horror, in tandem.

"I'm with Cat on this. Can't you turn this shit off for one night?"

"Language, Charles. There's a baby in the room," Colin chided. He turned to Catherine and leaned to kiss her on the forehead. "It won't be for long. We're in court Tuesday and I just need to review the court documents once more."

Catherine pouted but lifted her face to receive the kiss. "That's what you have paralegals for, Olly."

"I can call my mother to come back, if Huck can't stay," Colin said. He was already swinging his trench coat off the rack near the door.

"Please, God, no," Catherine whispered, loud enough only for Charles to hear.

"No, I'm already here," Charles said. "I'll stay."

"I'm not an invalid," Catherine protested.

"No, you are not that," Colin agreed, smiling, as he disappeared through the door.

"He's been paranoid about me ever since Carolina's ordeal with Clancy," Catherine said with a sigh. She leaned back into her chair. Oz snored softly in the bassinet a foot away. "But my delivery was *fine.* Early, but fine. Oz is healthy. I'm healthy. He's being ridiculous, and frankly, if he was that concerned, he would stay himself and not pawn me off on his best friend."

Charles pointed at the door. "I can leave, and we can say I stayed for a couple hours."

"Wouldn't be the first lie we told Colin," she said. Catherine pulled her hair up into a ponytail and clipped it with a quick dexterity that had him mesmerized. "No, stay for a bit. When's the last time we were alone together, anyway?"

When's the last time anything good came of us being alone? "He's beautiful," Charles said, because he couldn't think of a response to her question that didn't lead them down a dangerous path.

Catherine smiled. She snaked an arm over the chair and into the cradle. "He is, isn't he?"

"It looks good on you," Charles said. "Motherhood, or whatever."

"Or whatever?"

"Shit, Cat, I'm no good at small talk, or serious talk, or any of it." Charles rubbed his hands over the whisper of stubble on his chin. "Sorry for saying shit in front of the baby again."

"That's three times," she teased. "Besides, he hasn't even settled on his permanent eye color. What are the odds that shit becomes his first word?"

Charles laughed. "That would be fucking hilarious."

"Colin would love that." She withdrew her hand and folded it across her other, in her lap. "He's only grown more particular about things over time."

"Colin was never going to be a man who knows how to relax and have a good time."

"I thought marriage and fatherhood would soften him."

"You can't change anyone, Cat."

"You've changed."

Charles inhaled, but it did no good. What he needed was a lungful of smoke. A bump of coke. "I've adapted."

"You make it sound so depressing. Isn't that what I've done, adapted?"

"Catherine, no one forced you to take this path. You chose to marry Colin, and chose to have his child." No, not one bump. Twelve. Why had he agreed to this? "I don't know why you insist on acting like you're a martyr."

Her eyes teared. "I'm sorry you see me that way, as a foolish girl who can't appreciate that she caused her own circumstances."

Charles leaned forward over his knees. He clasped his hands together to avoid touching her. "I don't think that."

"It's what you said."

"I guess it is," Charles conceded. "It helps me to think it, when you chose him."

"You know why I chose him."

"I know what you told me. I know what you tell yourself so you can sleep at night."

"Who says I'm sleeping?"

Charles stood. "I'm gonna call Josephine. It wasn't a good idea for me to be here, alone with you."

"My marriage is failing, Huck." Catherine turned her head to the side, revealing a cheek full of tears. "And yes, I know why I chose him. And because of Oz, I would never choose differently. That doesn't change matters."

"If Colin were asked, would he say the same?"

Catherine laughed and sniffled at the same time. "Nothing is ever so complex for Colin. Nothing will ever be. He never did understand the value in dreaming."

"What's done is done," Charles said. Only now, when he'd stopped to take a deep breath, did he feel the tightness in his chest. The sensation of his heart breaking, again, a sensation only Catherine Connelly Sullivan could produce. "My advice is to think of your son now, Catherine. He's what matters. The rest is just details."

"Is that what you're going to do? Think of your son?"

"He's the only thing keeping me going," Charles said. He reached for the phone. "Should I call someone?"

"No."

"You'll be okay?"

"Yes, *Colin,* I'll be fine."

"I'm nothing like him, Catherine."

"Oh, I know," she replied, turning away from both her love and her son. "I'm reminded of that every single day."

Charles willed himself to move toward the door. To not go to her instead and take her in his arms, shake the sense into her, all the while kissing her, loving her. She was intoxicating and maddening, perfect and imperfect. His and not his. He loved her, he hated her. She was his salvation and his undoing.

"Be happy," he said before disappearing into the New Orleans night.

CHAPTER 2
Say You Love Me

Evangeline napped under the wall of ivy. She'd found it by accident, the lone brick behemoth speckled in green flora. It backed against a campus parking lot no one used anymore, and so no one used the wall, either, and once she'd found it, she'd staked her claim. Studying, meditating, reading, napping. It had many uses.

Massachusetts was everything she thought it would be, but more, it was everything she needed. It wasn't home, but there was no going home for Evangeline until she could learn to be her own person, able to separate her personal truth from the things that had happened to her. Where better to learn that than amongst like-minded scientists searching for the same truths?

Augustus said he wasn't mad, but Evangeline knew he was wounded by her choice to stay in New England for the summer. It wasn't that she didn't want to see her family… except, in a way, it was. Her family reminded her too much of all that had happened, and of an Evangeline who was incomplete. Damaged. She needed some separation from this, before she could risk letting this old feeling take over.

It wasn't an easy decision not to join the family for the summer reunion. She desperately wanted to meet her new niece and nephew, but she didn't want to meet them in her current frame of mind. When she first held their wiggling bodies, she wanted to appreciate it in a way she could appreciate very little right now.

She was both numb, and alive, and the former contributed to the latter.

No, this was where Evangeline belonged. Where equations and measurements and theories ruled supreme. Where she could be who she was born to be and, Newton willing, discover who she was meant to be.

AUGUSTUS COULD HARDLY PROCESS THE NEWS.

He'd, of course, assumed this would come eventually. It was the natural evolution of a new marriage; of the intimacy between man and wife. He hadn't thought too far ahead on what being a father would mean for him, because he was afraid to want it too much. The success of his business lay solidly in the column of things he could control. When there, he could think and piece together a plan that reached far into the future.

He had learned very, very early in his short marriage that his wife—and all that came with her, from her erratic moods to her strange whims—was far beyond his control. The child growing within her, then, was an extension of that nebulous part of his life that both thrilled and frightened Augustus.

Ekatherina slept in the hospital bed, hooked up to a series of monitors sounding varying beeps that no one bothered to explain. She'd fainted earlier that day, at the office, and Augustus rushed her to Charity Hospital as fast as his car would carry them. The doctor ran a series of tests and returned with a smile and the news.

"There's nothing wrong with your wife, Mr. Deschanel. To the contrary! She's expecting."

"Expecting what?"

The doctor blinked, regarding him strangely. "Why, expecting a child. What else?"

"A child. A baby?"

"Can I get you something, Mr. Deschanel? Some water, perhaps?"

"No, no. I'm... fine. When is the baby due?"

"Her obstetrician will be the best person to give you that information, but I'd say, anywhere from six to twenty weeks."

Augustus frowned. He wrapped his hands into fists in his pockets. There was a big difference between six and twenty weeks, that went well beyond time, in their case. Six weeks meant... twenty meant... "That's a huge spread, doctor."

He sighed, then smiled. "As I said, I'm not the expert where this is concerned."

"Wouldn't she be showing a lot more if she was twenty weeks along?"

The doctor shrugged. "She's a smaller gal, and they can sometimes go full term without more than a slight bump. Again, I'm not the right person to give advice on this, and I think it's best to collect your questions for the obstetrician."

"I see." Augustus ran his hands over his face. "Then maybe you can tell me why she passed out?"

"She's dehydrated, so we'll keep her on fluids for a few hours before we release her. I'll prescribe a vitamin regimen, and I'd advise a short walk each evening, to keep her blood flow healthy. Do you know anything about the women in her family? Any medical history?"

Augustus shook his head. "No, but I can ask her when she wakes."

"She may also be low on potassium, and there's some signs she might... well, that's premature. We'll leave that to her obstetrician. I can make some recommendations."

"Thanks," Augustus said, though he'd call the Sullivans later. They'd found the best for Catherine, Cordelia, and Maureen, and Augustus wanted the same for his wife.

Ekatherina stirred, slowly waking. His heart raced at the thought of even more complications ahead. This doctor had implied there was something else wrong, but lacked the backbone or experience to put words to the ailment.

"Hi," he said when she rolled her head to look at him.

"Husband."

"Were you awake when the doctor gave us the news?"

Ekatherina turned her head away. "A baby, he say?"

"Yes. It's wonderful news," Augustus said.

"As you say, husband."

She tugged the blanket over her head, dismissing the conversation.

Two days they'd been home, and Ekatherina hadn't left her bed except to use the bathroom. Augustus stayed home to see to it she followed doctor's orders, but while she seemed recovered from the brief physical assault, some new malaise had settled over her, and this was even more crippling.

"Why don't we try a walk?" he asked at dusk. Ekatherina rolled away from him and tucked her blanket under her chin in response.

Try as he did, Augustus didn't understand her. He didn't understand how she could be, in one moment, his angel of succor and mercy, and in another, distant and far, far away. Had she been like this with George Cairne, those months alone on Summer Island?

Stop. Only a fool obsesses over such things. Augustus paced the long upstairs hall, dwelling when he should be solving. Stalling when he should be working.

I'd say, anywhere between six to twenty weeks.

Augustus didn't need to do the math to understand the implications of twenty weeks.

He'd scheduled her obstetrician, but Ekatherina refused to go see him. She insisted her mammochka never had one, and she didn't need anything that her mammochka didn't need.

Elizabeth, who'd been by earlier cashing in on Augustus'

promise to help her practice driving, remarked that Ekatherina needed help.

"I'm not talking about a doctor, Aggie."

"Then what kind of help, exactly?" Augustus asked, already on the way to being annoyed at the unsolicited remark.

"Maybe the kind Colleen and Evangeline offer," she said.

"That would be great, if either of them were *here*."

Elizabeth shrugged, which was so very like her when discussing anything serious. He supposed she had her defense mechanisms, as he had his. "Yeah, well, call 'em. You never know."

Augustus spoke with Colleen first, though it took him another two days to make the call. To ask her to use her ability, when he'd made quite clear his unwillingness to use his own, felt a betrayal of his moral code. But Colleen had never shared his reservations. She never hesitated to heal someone in need and never seemed to carry around any baggage about the choice after.

"Aggie," she said, after she listened to him tell as much of the tale as he could tell. He left out the parts he couldn't bear to speak aloud, like the words George Cairne. "What you're describing isn't something either Evangeline or I are capable of healing. We heal the physical… draw matter back into place, and focus on seeing it whole. If we could heal the mind? Well, we'd be miracle workers."

"I never said her mind needed healing, Colleen."

"My dear, you didn't need to." She hesitated and then said, "I'm so happy for you. Seems our family will be welcoming three little ones this year."

"Will you be home this summer, or not?"

"I will, and of course I'll come see Ekatherina, but… I don't want to disappoint you."

"You won't," he said and hung up before her pity seeped further into his marrow, where the other bad thoughts threatened to take hold.

. . .

THAT NIGHT, AUGUSTUS DREAMED OF A BEAMING Ekatherina, dancing in the arms of George Cairne, on and on until they reached the ocean, gliding across the waves.

AUGUSTUS WENT TO SEE HIS MOTHER THE FOLLOWING day. Irish Colleen often accused him of never needing her, but that wasn't true. Being in her presence was often enough to ground him and bring him back to a simpler time, one she'd brought to their complex lives. One where bread baking could heal a broken heart, and a mother's touch was enough to dull the pain of a wound.

He told her first of their good news, and then, tentatively, approached the subject of Ekatherina's struggles.

"Oh dear," Irish Colleen said. She wrinkled her face and settled her rag over one arm. "Poor thing is probably missing her mother. Nothing can be done about that, I suppose."

"No," Augustus agreed. "I've tried. I have to return to work, but I can't leave her when she's like this."

"If anyone could make that happen, it's you," she said, patting his arm. "I'm more than happy to attend her, but I think a replacement mother might be worse than none. A woman is predisposed to resent her mother-in-law, you know."

Augustus nodded.

"How about Elizabeth? She's ahead in her studies, and she could spend her afternoons there, so you could return to work. Evenings, too, if she stays ahead."

Elizabeth agreed, in return for more driving practice. *I'll even stay the night, as long as you get me back here in the morning for my studies. Wouldn't want to piss off the banshee.*

Augustus would have given her more than driving practice, for the peace of mind he'd receive in return.

"As for her refusing a doctor..." Irish Colleen clucked her tongue. "Well, that's just foolish, and frankly, childish. She doesn't have a choice where your child's health and development are concerned. If she won't go see the doctor, you call him and make *him* come see *her.*"

AUGUSTUS RELUCTANTLY RETURNED TO WORK THE following day. Word of their good news had already spread around the office, and he fielded good wishes with mounting anxiety. It wasn't good news. It should be good news, but there was so much shrouding it.

Ekatherina's refusal to speak to him.

The unknown.

Twenty weeks.

He sat through an executive staff meeting and managed to say the right things, but after, he locked himself in his office and closed his eyes.

He saw Ekatherina, but she wasn't alone.

George Cairne swept her across the sea, her blue dress trailing behind her like a wisp of smoke.

Augustus opened his bottom drawer. Inside lay the remnants of wedding gifts from his employees, at least those they hadn't found use for at the house. Most of what was left would never be used, but there were three bottles of liquor he'd kept around, just in case. In case of a celebration. In case one of his employees had their own good news to share.

In case of twenty weeks.

Augustus broke the seal on a bottle of two-hundred-year-old Scotch and took a long swallow. The liquor was bracing, and it burned everywhere, setting his throat and chest aflame. He pressed his hand to his lips to prevent himself from expelling it all over his desk.

Then, he walked to the break room and turned the vintage bottle upside down over the sink. He focused on his breathing as he poured the remaining amber contents down the drain.

CHAPTER 3
Landslide

Maureen winced with every flicker of lightning. The storm lit the dark house with each powerful flash, followed quickly by the deafening crash of thunder that was coming far too quickly now. A peek out the heavy burgundy curtains revealed exactly what she expected to find: A flooded street. Floods in New Orleans, which sat at and in some cases below sea level, brought things out of the ground. Things that had no business being above the earth, like the dead. And there were still cemeteries in the area who buried their dead, rather than entombing them, because the tombs were for those wealthy enough to afford that protection for their heavenly rest.

She hated storms. Always had. She'd make an exception for snow, because they experienced it so rarely in South Louisiana, but the rain cast a depressing pall over life that was hard to overcome. Nine months pregnant, this was the last thing Maureen needed when she was already in a near permanent daze, as she approached the half-year mark in her tenure as mistress of Blanchard House.

That's what the staff called her. Mistress Blanchard. She supposed it sounded enough like Miss Havisham to both light something familiar and mischievous within her, but also served as a reminder of who she might one day become. What possible future awaited a woman in a loveless marriage? She'd be a mother soon, and she looked forward to that. But her life as a woman was effectively over.

The next bout of lightning came with a consuming pain in her lower abdomen. Maureen doubled over at the acute attack and struggled for a moment to breathe. This wasn't her first pain of the day, but it was, by far, the worst. Her doctor had said she would have minor contractions in the weeks nearing her quickening, but she'd zoned out at some point in his lectures and couldn't remember what he'd said about what to do when they were no longer minor, or far apart.

Edouard wouldn't be home for hours. If this storm continued the way it was going, he might not be home at all, because there were stretches of St. Charles Avenue that had poor drainage and were already flooded. Twice already this season, he'd called home to say he was taking a room at the Roosevelt and would be home in the morning, when it was safe to drive.

It was unusual for them to have so many strong spring storms, and Maureen thought, as she gripped the mahogany banister when her knees buckled from the pain, that perhaps it was the heavens crying for her lost potential.

She hadn't seen any of her family since she moved out of her mother's house. Not even on Christmas, which was a fine punishment for the isolation they'd gifted her with this solution to her newest "problem." But then Colleen had gone and ruined it by staying in Scotland for Christmas, and Charles remained sequestered in his old plantation, and so Maureen's message fell flat.

Mama called almost every day, and the staff had their refrain down pat now. *Mistress Blanchard is indisposed. May I take a message?* They said the same to Elizabeth, and Augustus, when they called. Colleen only wrote letters, for she was clearly *far* too busy and important to spare a call to her pitiful, married sister wasting her life in a rotting St. Charles mansion.

Charles called, too, but of all of them, she felt the least forgiving toward her oldest brother. He was the only one, not just of the Deschanels, but anyone, who knew her burden. Her secret.

Not that her secret was much of anything now. The dead hadn't visited her in many months. She didn't know if they ever would again, nor how she felt about this. At times, she wondered if she'd imagined the whole thing. The whims of an over-imaginative child.

Something tingled between her legs, followed by a rush of liquid. She hadn't urinated on herself; she'd know, because that felt very different from this expelling of water, which dumped out of her in a whoosh, pooling at her slippered feet.

"Shit." The word formed slowly, realization dawning with each letter. "Oh, oh, shit. Oh, *no.*" She clamped her hand around a nearby bell, but before she went to ring it, she stopped, remembering there would be no one to hear the sound. Today was Sunday, and the staff had the day off for worship, or whatever else they did when they weren't stoically tending to the needs of the Blanchards.

Maureen crumpled into a careful heap near the desk in the corner of the parlor. Reaching her hand up blindly, she found the phone and tugged it until it landed in her hands. She focused her heavy breaths, in, out, inhale, release, as her fingers tugged the rotary dial. Edouard worked every Sunday, because he liked the office to himself. It would be him and his secretary only. If Sheila wasn't old as dirt and ugly to boot, Maureen might have had some things to say about that.

"Sheila, put Edouard on. Now," Maureen commanded. She rarely called, as per his very clear orders when they were first married, but this more than qualified for *emergency*.

"Mrs. Blanchard. Yes, let me find him. One moment."

Maureen heard the secretary put the phone down, but then another sound replaced it.

Silence.

"Hello?" Maureen smacked the receiver. "Hello?"

Nothing. Not the subtle ambience of a background in subdued action. Not anything at all.

Maureen pressed the two buttons on the receiver. Nothing. No dial tone. She slammed her fingers down as the panic rose over her; as she began to understand what was happening to her and that it was happening when she was completely alone.

"Maybe he'll come home early," she whispered, but he never did, because Edouard had nothing worth coming home *to.*

The next crash of lightning fried the electricity. The whistling hum of the power leaving the fixtures and appliances sounded like the very last of her hope dying.

More pain rocked through her. Maureen grasped her belly, heaving desperately and awkwardly through the breathing exercise she'd practiced so many times but now couldn't quite remember how to perfect. *Don't think. Don't think about being alone. About the power and phone being out. About having this baby, here, on this hundred-year-old carpet your husband's great-grandmother picked out.*

"Hell's bells, Olivia. Does it have to be now?" Maureen asked, splayed unnaturally as she leaned against the old desk. Most of the furniture in this house was old and dour, but she appreciated the sturdiness of the hard wood. It was the nearest she had to strength, and it reminded her that she wasn't *entirely* alone. She still had her wits. A roof over her head. This could be worse.

Maureen's eyes filled with stars as a new pain gripped her. This one demanding, insistent. "No," she whispered. "No, not now. *Please* not now."

She scanned the room, searching for something, anything. But what? What could there possibly be *here,* in this mausoleum, to help her bring a child into the world?

Nothing. The answer was nothing, and the question didn't matter anymore. Maureen was not the smartest, or most interesting, or most promising of the Deschanel children, but she was easily the most resourceful. She'd held tight to this mantle of survivorship, because, often, it was all she had. All she knew about herself that mattered.

Time to think, Maureen Amelia. What do you know?

I know I'm all alone in this house.

I know the power is out, but I still have hours of daylight.

I know the phone lines are down, and it could be days before they get to them.

I know Edouard won't be home in time for his presence to matter.

I know if I open my door and scream, there's a very real risk that I might attract someone who will make this worse.

I know this child is coming soon.

I know I am a Deschanel.

"I know I am a Deschanel," Maureen whispered into the dark room. Dark, despite the light outside, because that was how her husband liked it. Dark, though her husband wasn't here, and she was.

Madeline was the one who taught Maureen and Elizabeth the trick. Colleen had gotten mad and wanted no part in it, and Evangeline did whatever Colleen wanted. But Madeline, who'd always had a taste for what was beyond far more than what was here, had discovered a pretty cool ability. One, she insisted, they all had.

Mama was mad, and I wished for Daddy. I wished so hard that when he came home an hour later, he said he heard my wish in his head.

How many hours had the three of them practiced this trick? First spreading out across Oak Haven, and later, trying it again when they were each in their classrooms. Years, it had been, since Maureen tried this, but she remembered the sensation, the intent, and the result.

Was it possible now?

And if so, who would she call?

Elizabeth never thought she'd see the day where she wished for her visions over reality. The visions were a known quantity. When she saw something, it happened. Nothing she could do about that, and while that was horrible and helpless, there was, she realized now, some small comfort in knowing she couldn't fix it.

In knowing there was no potential for trying and failing to make right what was about to go unstoppably wrong.

When she sat with Ekatherina, she found herself frustrated. Ekatherina's stubborn refusal to rise from bed, when she was clearly not that unwell, at least not physically, was only made worse by the lack of visions showing Elizabeth what was even going on with this strange young woman. It didn't make it easier that Ekatherina hardly acknowledged her presence. No hello when Elizabeth planted herself at her sister-in-law's bedside. No goodbye when she either retired for bed or home. The only sign a person existed inside her was the glimmer of recognition, and sometimes some other emotion—hostility, anger, resignation—when she accepted her meals on the old silver tray.

What the hell was I thinking?

You were thinking you needed driving lessons, and your brother needed you.

Elizabeth cracked open her physics textbook with a sigh. She hated physics, but at least it was quiet here. She didn't have to listen to her mother poorly explain something she didn't even remotely understand as she ruined her youngest daughter's education with the best intentions.

It's not so hard, Connor said once. *Whatever goes up, must come down. Unless you're, you know, in zero gravity.*

Elizabeth sipped her fizzy Coke and tried not to think of Connor. He promised to be there for her, and he had been, but it wasn't his fault his mother was diagnosed with cancer and needed all of her husband's focus. He didn't ask to be shipped off to his aunt's house, with his twin brother, Thomas, for the foreseeable future, where he had a license, but no car, and no way to come see Elizabeth no matter how badly he wanted to.

Lizzy, this is killing me. You need me, and I'm stuck here. I can't even sleep, I'm so upset about it.

Connor... your mother needs your patience more than I need you. It will be okay. Don't worry.

I'm supposed to be saying that to you.

He got one call a week, because his aunt didn't like the phone lines tied up. She never explained why, but the one time he tried to sneak a second call into Elizabeth, he got a switch to his palms, and that was that.

"Aunt Edith is very old-fashioned," he explained on his next call, and they both shuddered.

Elizabeth hadn't touched the drugs since the day Connor escorted her to the methadone clinic. She'd wanted a way out, despite the reprieve drugs like heroin offered, but hadn't known how to ask. But the adjustment to her system had left her an insomniac, so she'd shuffled down to the grocer and picked up a sleep aid. It wasn't very strong, the pharmacist said, but should be fine for a kid. He'd winked, as if he had any idea how she'd come to this point. Probably thought she was hitting the books too hard.

"Thanks for telling me," Connor said, when she did. She wouldn't lie to him. Not anymore, not ever again. "I guess there's no harm in it. I mean, they sell them at Schwegmann's, right?"

They helped, at least where the sleep was concerned. And a rested Lizzy could handle the day better than a sleepy, miserable one.

Ekatherina stirred. She turned over in the bed, facing Elizabeth's direction. Elizabeth put her thumb over the page she was reading and looked up.

Ekatherina was looking right at her.

"Where my husband?"

"Augustus is at work," Elizabeth said. The words came harder than words normally came. What if she said the wrong thing, even if it was right? Ekatherina was fragile in ways none of them had yet even begun to comprehend. That much the visions *had* told her. "Want me to call him?"

"No."

"I can ask him to come home early."

"He would be angry."

Elizabeth chuckled. "At you? No."

"What day is?"

"Uh... Tuesday, I suppose. Yeah. Tuesday. Do you have an appointment?"

Ekatherina curled her arms into the folds of the blanket. "He make me see doctor I don't want to see. My mammochka never need doctor. I don't need doctor."

Elizabeth set her book aside. Outside, the storm gathered momentum, and the rain thundered so loud she had to raise her voice. "Catherine, women still *die* in this country from childbirth complications. Even now, in the twentieth century. The United States still has one of the highest mortality rates for women in delivery." She didn't know why she'd said it. It was some fact Evangeline had dropped on them at the dinner table one night, clearing the rest of the meal for any normal conversation.

Ekatherina scoffed. "What is meant to be will be. We are not God."

"God gave us our intelligence, and that intelligence created life-saving medical procedures," Elizabeth argued, still channeling her older sister. "God wouldn't want us to be stupid with the gifts He gave us."

She realized her error as soon as she said it.

"You think me stupid?"

Elizabeth sighed. She was no good at this. Of all the Deschanel women, she was the least equipped for a conversation like this. "No, I think you're... I don't know, scared. But you're giving birth to a Deschanel, and, like it or not, that means you're gonna get the best medical care our ridiculous amounts of money can buy. I'm sure your mammochka is a real badass, but we're not taking chances with Augustus' kid."

"Badass? You think my mammochka a bad person?"

Elizabeth shook her head. "No, no, look, it's a compliment. It means she's tough. I'm just saying—"

Elizabeth's words came to a sudden halt. She lost them to a new sensation. An intrusion, one she hadn't felt since... since....

She swallowed. Lightning crashed outside and the room was bathed in shocking light. Ekatherina watched her in anticipation, but Elizabeth needed to focus, because she wasn't completely, totally sure, except...

Maureen.

Maureen needs me.

Maureen is in trouble.

Could it be? Was it possible? They'd abandoned the neat little parlor trick when Irish Colleen found out and grounded them for practicing their abilities in school. So many years had passed, but their abilities had only strengthened, so of course they could still do it, of course...

Lizzy, the baby is coming.

"Something is wrong," Ekatherina said, reading her face. "What is wrong?"

"Nothing, I just..." Elizabeth set her book aside. The feeling only grew stronger, this sense that Maureen was having her baby, and she needed her. Needed her *now.* "You'll be okay if I have to leave for a bit?"

Ekatherina coughed out a proud laugh. "I no need anyone, Elizabeth. Husband thinks he know best and only make it worse."

"Sure, okay, and I'll be back, it's just..." *Maureen. The baby is coming.*

And why would Maureen send for her in this way? Why not call?

The phone lines. Elizabeth reached for the phone at Ekatherina's bedside and there was nothing, not even a dial tone.

"Shit."

"What is it?"

"Nothing."

"You Deschanels. You love secrets."

"Yeah, I wouldn't say we love them, exactly." *Think. Without a phone you can't call the hospital. Can't send for help. What else can you do?*

Ekatherina's car was in the back. The keys dangled by the back door. Elizabeth couldn't legally drive, but that hadn't stopped her before, and if there was ever a time for her to break the rules, it was now.

"I'll be back," Elizabeth said and shot out of her seat and out the door, before her sister-in-law could ask any more questions.

OLIVIA BLANCHARD WAS BORN FIVE SECONDS AFTER THE stroke of midnight. Maureen was not awake the moment Irish Colleen brought her swaddled daughter for her to hold. She'd passed out from the pain as soon as she heard the reassuring song of Olivia's first cries.

When she awoke, she struggled to put the past hours together. She remembered the beam of light cast across the old, musty carpets, and the excruciating second before she saw who had come to save her.

Her mother. With Elizabeth in tow.

Maureen had half a mind to demand Elizabeth explain why she'd brought that wretched woman and not a doctor, but the wide-eyed terror in her baby sister's eyes told the story: Elizabeth had intercepted her call for help and went to the first place—first, last, in between—she thought of, because it was the one place they'd always been safe.

Their mother had delivered children into the world before, for others. She'd nursed their father's first wife through her tumultuous final days, as the cancer turned her into a stranger. She had never shown the tender care of a nursemaid to her own children, claiming she had a responsibility to harden them for a hard world ahead, but she would give this tender side to Maureen now, when she truly needed it.

"Mama," she'd cried and then passed out for the first time.

She'd awoken next in bed. Not hers, but a bed in one of their spare rooms, and though her mother didn't explain her choice, Maureen appreciated the practical decision. Edouard might never forgive her for ruining her own bed, or his. Irish Colleen blurred in and out of focus at her side, her strong hands ringing rags in the copper bin on the bedside table. Maureen saw this version of her mother as the embodiment of love. Then, Irish Colleen broke the reverie with barked orders at Elizabeth for more towels and a refresh on the hot water.

"I'm afraid, Mama," Maureen admitted, and she wasn't sure she'd ever said those words aloud to anyone in earnest, ever. But she'd never known such exquisite physical pain; never, ever been pushed so far to the brink that she feared the abyss beyond. "What if I die here? What if my baby dies?"

"Hush, now, sweet girl. No one is dying here today."

"Don't I need to be in a hospital?"

"No time," Elizabeth said, in a harried tone as she dropped the pile of clean towels at the end of the bed. "Tante Ophelia told Mama that Deschanels drop their babies *fast*."

"What?" Maureen winced through another powerful contraction.

"Your child is coming soon, dear," Irish Colleen said as she mopped at her brow. "Within hours of your water break. Some women toil in labor for a day or more. Not Deschanel women."

"It hurts so much, Mama. I just want to close my eyes..."

"You can close your eyes when the work is done, Maureen. If you want your daughter to arrive safely, you must be the one to bring her in. Awake."

"What if I can't?"

"I brought nine into this world, and seven went on to give me penance for my sins, so, yes, Maureen Amelia, you *can*."

OLIVIA'S SOFT COOS WOKE MAUREEN. IRISH COLLEEN had rested the baby upon her chest, but didn't remove her own hands until she saw Maureen had come to her senses again.

The well behind her eyes burst. She was overcome. There was nothing, not in her past, not in her future, that would ever dull the wholly complete joy coursing through her at the feel of her daughter's soft, pliant skin against hers; at the sound of a song meant only for her.

Maureen wasn't the same. She'd never be who she was again, and she would never wish for anything beyond what lay in her arms.

"Olivia," she whispered, and even her voice was no longer her own.

Olivia's tiny, fragile feet kicked with thoughtless abandon. Her little mouth puckered.

"Thank you, Mama," Maureen whispered, closing her own eyes so she could find herself lost with wherever her daughter's simple thoughts went. She'd long forgotten how she'd sworn never to speak to her mother, or any of the family, ever again. It didn't matter anymore. Olivia had changed everything. Everything, absolutely everything.

"I'll schedule the christening," Irish Colleen responded and collapsed into the doorframe.

CHAPTER 4

Love Hurts

Charles lifted his beer with a widening grin. Augustus frowned, paused, then raised his own glass with a careful smile.

"What are we toasting?" Augustus asked.

"The first time we've ever had lunch together."

Augustus clinked his glass against his brother's. "Unless you count the thousands of times over the years growing up."

Charles took a deep swallow and licked his lips. "Just the two of us, I mean."

"There was a time, you know, when it was only the two of us. Before the girls."

"You being cute, Augustus?"

"This is me you're talking about."

"True enough." Charles finished his beer and slid it to the edge of the table. The wait staff at Galatoire's were used to his whims and knew not to take too long in refilling Charles Deschanel's drinks. "First time as men, though," he seemingly couldn't help adding.

"Hopefully not the last."

Augustus meant the words. Growing up, he and Charles had ebbed and flowed through varying levels of closeness; inseparable as toddlers and little boys, growing further apart as their developing personalities carried them in different directions. Augustus loved his sisters but had always wanted a brother he could relate to, and at times, confide in. In his late teens, he'd accepted that he would never get that, not from Charles, but in the past year they'd found common ground, and that was enough. Their unhappy marriages bound them, and their love of family was the glue.

"You wanted advice," Charles began. He closed the menu and set it aside. Looking at it had been an exercise in pointlessness. He always ordered the shrimp and grits, despite that they were at one of the nicest restaurants in New Orleans and he could get shrimp and grits at any restaurant in the city.

"I don't know if I want advice or a sounding board," Augustus began, carefully. "First, this is between us. I don't need Mama, or the girls, nagging at me about this, or offering their own advice. It won't help."

Charles folded his hands. "Okay. Between us."

Augustus swirled the wine in the glass, his index and middle finger perched at the base of the stem, guiding the movement. He'd aerated this wine into oblivion. He didn't much like wine, or any alcohol, but it seemed a far less offensive drink to order at noon than spirits or beer. A red wine was what he ordered on business lunches, sipping it with polite interest, but without any real enjoyment. "I'm not positive the child Ekatherina is carrying is mine."

With the words finally out, Augustus felt worse, not better.

Charles' eyes widened. He tapped his empty beer glass against the table without taking his gaze off his brother. "That motherfucker in Maine, you mean."

"Yes." Augustus wouldn't say his name. It had no place in their lives.

"But she's been home for a while now. Wouldn't her due date make it obvious?"

Augustus set his jaw. "That's the thing, Huck. She won't *see* a doctor. When she was admitted to the ER, the hack doctor there said she could be anywhere from six to twenty weeks."

"Well, shit, I don't need an expensive degree to make a forecast like that."

"That's what I said."

"But why the hell doesn't she want to see a doctor?" Charles accepted his refilled beer and inhaled the scent before washing more of it back. "Unless you think she's afraid it will tell the wrong story?"

"I don't know what Ekatherina's reasons are," Augustus said. "Where she comes from, a good doctor is a luxury her family never had. But this is a *child* we're talking about, and her laissez faire approach to the baby's life is worrying me. She's not even... she won't even get out of bed."

"Lizzy still staying with her?"

"For now, but I can't ask her to stay forever."

"Well, the baby will either be born sooner or later, depending on what end of the quack's prediction was right."

"Not funny."

"No," Charles agreed. "Not funny. But neither is this bullshit she's pulling. Look, I know you love her, as you should. I wish I knew that feeling toward my own wife. Sounds nice. But Aggie, she doesn't have a *choice* where the doctor is concerned. Unless she plans to get rid of this baby, she's gotta take care of herself."

"I know, that's why I have a doctor coming to the house tomorrow," Augustus admitted reluctantly. He'd promised his wife she would marry a man with no expectations of her, and he'd broken that promise more than once.

"Good man."

"I don't feel good about it. I feel sick."

"But you'll have answers."

"And what if the answer is the one I'm dreading, Huck? What then?"

Charles bowed his head over his drink with a frown. He appeared to give the question very serious consideration. "I don't know. What do you want?"

"I want my wife to be herself again. I want this child to be mine."

"And if neither of those happen?"

Augustus couldn't answer. He couldn't even fathom such a future.

"You've got a doctor coming. You'll have answers tomorrow," Charles said. "Answers you can use to decide what the hell to do next. But, you know, you could have asked one of the girls to lay hands on Ekatherina. Evangeline did that with Cordelia, though Cordelia had no idea she was being anything other than sisterly. It's why I know I'm having a boy. She, or even Lizzy, could tell you right off the bat if the baby is yours, and what he or she will be. Something to consider."

"I shouldn't trust the doctor, is that what you're saying?"

"After the one who gave you the kind of odds a bookie would laugh at?"

"Right." Augustus dipped his spoon into his soup, then realized he wasn't hungry at all. "I could ask Lizzy."

"Should ask her. She'd do it. Hell, maybe already has, and just hasn't told you, because you haven't asked."

"Your son," Augustus said. "Have you picked a name?"

"I have. And you might say it was inspired by your wife."

"Sorry?"

"I picked a fine Russian name. Russian royalty. Those Russkies have a hell of a lot of courage, and backbone. I don't know what Ekatherina was up to all those months in Maine, but I know she never apologized for it, did she? Well, that might not be what I want for my wife, but I want it for my boy. I want him to come into this world a force of nature and remain in it by not tolerating any of the bullshit the world throws at him. I want him to take what he wants, no matter what others think or say. He's a Deschanel, and he has the whole world in his reach."

"What does Cordelia think?"

"What she thinks," Charles said, mouth full of shrimp, "is really not a damn thing to me."

. . .

After lunch, Charles stopped by to see his mother. She'd left a message at Ophélie, asking him to come see her whenever it was convenient. Charles knew that "whenever it was convenient," meant that if he wasn't there before dinner, he'd failed as a son.

The week before, he'd stopped by and brought her a piece of new technology: A VHS machine. He purchased one for Ophélie, and on a whim, bought one for his mother, who loved old movies. She stared at it as if it contained alien intelligence, blinked a few times, and then asked him what in heaven she was supposed to do with it.

"Watch movies, Ma."

"And just when do I have time to watch movies?"

Charles resisted the urge to remind her she only had one child in the house nowadays, because the whole point in bringing the newfangled machine to the house was to cheer her up and remind her there were other things she could do to keep her spirits up.

He fully expected this visit to be her insisting he return it to the electronic store, but she didn't mention the movie machine at all. She had something else entirely on her mind.

"Before you say no, hear me out," Irish Colleen said, but she needn't have bothered. Her offer to find them a nanny made sense in every way. Charles would need the help, no question, and Cordelia was about as maternal as a fire ant.

"I was thinking," she went on, when she'd won the initial battle, hedging despite his easy acquiescence, "that I could send her over to you now. Early, before your son is born. That way, she can get to know everyone, and you can feel comfortable with the woman who will be seeing after your children. It's an important job. You should have time to make sure she's a good fit for your family."

"Yeah, sure." Charles didn't know why his mother was selling this so hard. "I assumed we'd hire a nanny anyway."

"Wonderful! I'll call her mother and let her know!"

"Her mother?"

"Yes, dear. She still lives at home with her mama. Not all families are as fortunate as we are. But she's quite young and full of energy, and will be perfect."

"You've met her? What's her name?"

"Lisette. Lisette Duchene, and I should tell you, her English is not the best. She grew up in France, in some poor countryside town, God bless them, and they've been in America only a few short years. But would it not be splendid for your son to learn your father's family's language?"

HE FOUND CORDELIA IN THE DOUBLE PARLOR. SHE'D taken it upon herself, as mistress of the house, to divide the parlor into two halves, one for ladies, one for men. It was a very traditional setup, one that hadn't been in place for generations, but Cordelia found her comfort, perhaps her only comfort, in the confines of what was proper.

She was reading from the Bible, though he'd never known her to be religious, or even attend church.

"Husband," she said with a cordial nod, without looking up.

"Hey, have a minute?"

"I can't make a child until the one growing inside me is no longer growing inside of me," came her clipped reply.

"Not *that*," he said and sat down across from her. The instinct to ask her permission was both strong and annoying. This was his house, and yet she'd encroached upon it in a hundred tiny ways that made him feel less connected to his familial land.

Cordelia pressed her thumb to hold her place, but didn't set the Bible aside. "I'm intrigued."

"I stopped by my mother's today, and she wants us to consider the nanny she's picked out for our son."

"I see."

"You're mad."

Cordelia grinned. "Not especially. A nanny is a practical choice, and I'd been considering it myself, except I know of no one I can ask. I have no mother to do this for me, and, of course no *father*, either—"

"Cordelia... I really am sorry for how that ended—"

"It's the past, Charles. The past is useless to us. We'll accept your mother's suggestion. Colleen was well-intentioned, of course."

Cordelia was the only person Charles knew who didn't call his mother Irish Colleen. This included everyone from the priests to their grocer.

"Great." Charles jumped to his feet, relieved to be done with the discussion.

"Wait. I have something for you as well."

With reluctance, he lowered himself back to the sofa. "What is it?"

This time, she did set the Bible aside. "I've been giving it serious thought, and I believe I'd like to sell my shares in my father's company to my brother."

Charles shrugged. "That's really your decision."

"I'd like your input."

Charles settled back into the couch. "You don't need the money, and seems like Darwin is doing a fine job of running your father's legacy into the ground. Probably wise to bail now, when there's still something to sell."

"Yes," Cordelia agreed. "I agree with all of that. But my reason goes deeper. I'd like to create some separation between my son and my brother. Darwin has a sense of family that goes beyond the practical, and I don't want him to use the business to gain leverage with our child as he grows into adulthood. Does that make sense?"

"Sort of." Charles didn't see the business lasting nearly that long.

"Darwin will continue to ask for money as long as we have any interest in the success of the business. If I sell off, or even surrender, my portion, he can no longer appeal to us with the premise of saving the business, because I'll no longer have any reason to see it saved."

Charles almost laughed. There existed not a single sentimental bone in his wife's body. Not even a small part of her wanted to see her father's business thrive simply because it had belonged to him. "I wasn't going to give him another fucking dime either way, but if it makes the denials easier for you."

"It does."

"Great. Feel free to use the Sullivans to handle the transaction."

"I will."

"Good. Good. They're good with things like this."

"I assumed as much."

"Colin Sr. especially. One time, he—"

Cordelia raised both brows in stern judgment. "Are we making small talk now, Charles?"

"Just thought maybe there was more to talk about."

"Should there be something else?"

Charles sighed. There would never be anything else. Anything resembling something warmer than a business transaction was a mountain too high. "I'll tell Mom to send Lisette over. Condoleezza can make up one of the guest suites. Maybe the one next to the nursery."

"Isn't it early for a nanny?"

"You're due any day now, Cordelia."

"Until then, her services aren't especially useful, though, are they?"

"Normally I'd agree," Charles said. "But Mama made a good point. We need to make sure she's a good fit, and better to figure that out *before* she has responsibility for the life and death of our son."

Cordelia tilted her head to the side. Her mouth twitched. "Yes, I see the advantage in this. Colleen gets it right from time to time." With both hands, she brushed the invisible dust off her skirt and rose in one stiff movement. "I'll see to the coordination here."

THE DOCTOR VISIT TO MAGNOLIA GRACE WAS NOT meant to be. Two hours before his scheduled arrival, Augustus jumped nearly to the ceiling at the sound of a knock at the front door.

Elizabeth flew down the stairs and past him in a flash, answering before he was even off the couch. He couldn't hear what she was saying, or who she was talking to.

"It's a telegram." She frowned and turned it over in her hand. "Do people still send these?"

"Yes, obviously, since we've received one," he said, taking it from her. She wore an indignant look as she was in the middle of reading the message.

Augustus read the short message five times. On each read, he tried to concoct some alternate message, some other way of interpreting what the words might mean. But there was only this:

News from home stop Please inform Ekatherina that her sister Anasofiya has moved into the arms of Our Lord stop She is no longer suffering stop There will be a brief service and so there is no need to travel home stop

Augustus ran his hand over his mouth. He looked up at Elizabeth. Elizabeth looked back and then snatched the small paper from his hand. He didn't stop her.

"Well, fuck," she said.

"Well, fuck," Augustus agreed. He turned toward the stairs. He couldn't tell her. He had to tell her. He had no right to keep such a thing from her.

"This isn't your fault, you know."

"Of course it isn't," he snapped, though he was already counting down his failures to bring Anasofiya to a country where she could have been seen by the best doctors his money could buy.

"What I mean, Aggie, is that I saw this in my visions, so it was always the way things were gonna go for your sister-in-law. You weren't meant to bring her here like a white knight and save her. So you can let go of that failure I know you have running through your head."

Both siblings' attentions were jerked to the ceiling at the sound of a primal wail.

"Seems like she already knows," Elizabeth said solemnly. "Maybe she's not so unlike us, after all."

AUGUSTUS HOVERED OUTSIDE HIS WIFE'S HOSPITAL room, trying as hard as he could to focus on what the doctor was telling him.

"Thirteen weeks," the obstetrician said. "Which, based on her records here, would have put her around five weeks when we saw her in April." He frowned. "You were told six to twenty?"

"Yes, that's what I was told."

"Odd." The doctor flipped through the chart as if his predecessor's incompetence would be explained in some way. "Well, Mr. Deschanel, the child is healthy, and your wife's levels are all healthy, but I worry about her stress. Both times, her ending up here appears to be caused by some inciting event. I understand she's received some distressing news today?"

I should never have left Russia! Never come here! Never marry! Never abandon them! I forget who I am!

"Yes, you could say that."

"We tried to calm her down, but she's completely insane," Elizabeth said, not so helpfully.

"This will be a long pregnancy if she can't learn to be calm," the doctor said. He closed the chart and looked directly at Augustus. "Your wife is perfectly healthy, Mr. Deschanel, but her mental constitution is such that any kind of excitement could send her back to the hospital. I wouldn't normally recommend bedrest so early in the term, but these episodes of your wife's are all a danger to the baby. Everything is fine now, but it could go another direction very quickly, if she can't keep her blood pressure down."

"When's the baby due?" Elizabeth asked.

The doctor smiled. "Christmas."

When he'd left them, Elizabeth turned to Augustus. "So, hey, I know you were worried the kid wasn't yours."

"What? How did you know that?"

She twitched the corner of her mouth into a smile. "Same way I know anything. But you can stop stressing over nothing. The baby's yours, Aggie. And if you don't wanna take the doctor's word for it, take mine. I put my hands on your wife, and I felt a Deschanel growing inside."

"Are you..." *Are you sure?* "Thanks, Elizabeth. You can go home now."

"Yeah. I'm sure," she answered the interrupted question. "I could tell you her name, but I think, on some level, you already know."

"Her? I'm going to have a daughter?"

Elizabeth smiled.

AUGUSTUS HOVERED OUTSIDE THE GLASS WINDOWS OF Ekatherina's hospital room. He should go in, but his feet were rooted into the old linoleum, and her reprisals from hours earlier still beat heartily in his head.

I should never have left Russia!

Never come here!

Never marry!

Never abandon them!

I forget who I am!

And the worst of all: *This baby is a curse.*

Augustus had grown up in a family whirl of superstition. He'd heard the word curse bandied about, mentioned in hushed whispers, and written upon documents. That most of his relatives believed in such a thing was testament to the power of a word. Once spoken, it was not easily forgotten.

He'd never been swept up in this frenzy of belief among Deschanels, but he now, finally, understood the weight of an utterance of such menace.

His wife believed their child was a curse, and so she was.

Augustus leaned against the wall and closed his eyes, searching for the strength that used to come to him with such ease.

CHAPTER 5

Tickets Home

Colleen slid the tickets in and out of the envelope. Home. The last time she saw New Orleans was Huck's wedding. The innate pull of belonging had lessened over time, until home became more of an abstract than something tangible and irreplaceable. Home shifted, became fluid, to the point where, when people asked her where she was from and she answered "Edinburgh," it no longer felt like an answer that required clarification.

She loved it here. She loved the old, fortressed city, with the brogue that warmed her soul and the foods that were comfortable year-round. The rolling green hills of the nearby Highlands called to her, and they were close enough to answer.

And here, at the northern end of this island across the Atlantic, which dipped into the North Sea, she was in love and there was nothing logical to defeat that. Not her own hang-ups, or the expectations of her family that were not theirs at all, but hers, projected onto them, glaring back at her like shining the sun into a mirror. Blinding.

Noah cleared her hair to the side and kissed the back of her neck. Chills rippled through her. She'd never welcomed intimacy before. She'd tolerated it, sometimes enjoyed it. She'd been in love, but never been in love with the *idea* of love, or all that came with it. Once, when she and Rory started dating, she even said as much out loud. *Why does love have to be so physical? Why not more cerebral?* Rory had only gaped at her.

Noah's touch brought her to life. A light that pulsed when he was closer and dimmed when he stepped away.

"Don't lose those," he warned. Home. Yes, she wanted to go, but not the way he did. His relationship with his father was more friend than child-parent, the two men having, in a way, raised each other in the absence of women. Noah radiated, looking ready to burst, at keeping such a secret from the person he'd been closest to his entire life. He was a superstitious man, too—where, Colleen wondered, did he get that?—and more than once expressed a fear that the universe would conspire to keep them from getting on the plane.

"Now that's just silly," Colleen had said, never adding that a part of her would welcome such a conspiracy from the fickle universe.

"Silly, okay, sure, let's just go make another offering to the fairies."

Colleen slipped the envelope back into the drawer. She paused as she went to close it.

"Why is this in here?" Colleen rotated her head back to him and was rewarded with a kiss, before Noah peered over her shoulder to glance into the contents.

His graduate degree, earned barely a month ago, rested in her hand. "I'll find a place for it later."

"Later? Noah, this is the culmination of everything you've ever worked for!"

Noah embraced her from behind, dropping his head on her shoulders. "It's part of it, sure."

"I don't understand."

"Everything came together for me in Edinburgh. Not only my education."

"Yes, but..."

"Besides." He kissed the hollow of her neck and her knees threatened to buckle. "No point in making holes in the walls of a place you're leaving. We'll have plenty of places to hang things in our new apartment. We're going to be late for the deposit."

The deposit! She glanced at the clock. They were meeting the broker in an hour. Colleen's eyes flew wide, as she catalogued everything that needed doing before they could leave. She was in her robe and pajamas still. The morning dishes sat in the sink, unwashed. The garbage would be collected later, and she hadn't gone through and consolidated every cannister into a single bag. Her bills were stacked in a neat pile by the door, but she'd yet to place stamps on them, and so she'd need to get to the post office to have them post them for her, if she didn't want to be late.

"I can almost see your mind whirring," he teased. "The scientist in me—"

Colleen spun, pecked him on the lips, lingering a half beat longer than she should have, with all that waited, and then rushed to complete the tasks needed to get them out the door on time to make their appointment.

The flat was a step down from the one Colleen had enjoyed for the past year. Unlike a home paid for through the trust, the options available to them on a budget set by the limitations of Noah's meager income were smaller and less appealing. Colleen reminded herself she hadn't come here to live like a princess. She smiled when Noah cast troubled eyes in her direction. She didn't need to read his mind. She knew what he was thinking.

"I still love it," she assured him, already thinking of ways she could make it more cozy. A fresh coat of paint, perhaps some heavy throw rugs. A pretty valance over the kitchen sink, overlooking a view that had likely driven the rent higher than it should have been. The emerald span Arthur's Seat gleamed beyond.

"Here's the deposit," Noah told the broker, handing him an envelope stuffed with cash. "And the contract, signed by us both."

"Thanks," the man said as he stuffed both into the interior pockets of his jackets. He checked his watch. "Sixty days."

"We can collect the keys in sixty days?"

"Aye."

"Should we set a date?" Noah asked.

"Aye. Sixty days."

Noah and Colleen exchanged looks. The man didn't waste words, that was for sure. They'd laughed about it one night, in the afterglow of love, wondering at what his wife must get from him in sex. *Yes. Go. Stop. More. Less.*

Colleen hid a smile. Noah tapped his thumb against his leg and asked if he had a calendar.

The man, who'd introduced himself when they first met as Ian, no last name offered, reached into the seemingly endless pocket of his blazer and extracted one.

He dropped it on the counter, flipped it open, and pointed.

"So, August tenth. Got it. Thanks," Noah said.

"Aye," said Ian and replaced the calendar, then, with a curt nod at them both, left. He stood outside the door and waited for them to follow. When they did, he locked the door behind them and lumbered off.

"If I didn't know better, I'd think he just wandered off the street and started charging people for properties that don't belong to him," Noah remarked.

"If not for that Rolex on his arm, I'd be inclined to agree."

"Sixty days." Noah whistled. "He talked so much I couldn't get a word in edgewise to ask why such a long wait."

Colleen laughed. "I remember his secretary telling us the owners had a few repairs to make."

"Who needs flushing toilets?"

"Or running water at all, for that matter?"

Noah impulsively wrapped his hands around her face and kissed her. He made a soft sound as he withdrew, pressing their foreheads together. "Sorry. I'll get better about letting us finish a conversation before being totally overcome by how much I love you," he said with a wry smile.

"Careful, I might be offended if I don't make you overcome in the future."

"Shit."

Colleen kissed him this time. Oh, what she wouldn't give to just stay here with him! To disappear into a life of obscurity, where who she was and where she'd come from was as inconsequential as the wars in countries she'd never visit. She cared about things too much, always had, but to disappear... to just disappear...

"Where'd you go?"

"What?"

"You went somewhere just now."

Unlike Rory, who took her tendency to ebb into deep thoughts as a personal affront, Noah was only curious. He asked questions designed to understand her better and was always amazed, never judging, or wondering why she couldn't be like others.

"I was thinking of how nice it would be to block the world out and just be."

Noah tucked a stray hair behind her ear, smoothing it into her hair with his fingertips. "I think that sometimes, too."

"Yeah?"

"Yeah."

"What is it about humans that we want what we don't have, but then, when we have what we wanted, we want something else? Or nothing at all?"

"Philosophy." Noah wrinkled his nose. "Who knows? We didn't evolve by being satisfied with what we had right in front of us, I suppose."

"I *am* satisfied with what's right in front of me," she said as she laced her hands into his. "Which is precisely why I'd like to disappear."

Noah's sigh was tender. "You're a worrier by nature." Not a judgment. Only an observation.

"I am, but it's more... it's...." The words came to her, and she realized them in the very moment they popped into her head; that she meant them. How true they were. "I've never seen anyone I know happy."

Noah's brows lifted. "None of you have ever been happy?"

"Not for long," she said, breaking the pause. "And my mother, I don't know if she's ever been happy either. She didn't marry for love, even if she did love my father."

"I guess I understand," Noah said. "My dad and I have been happy enough, but I know he misses my mother. I know he misses, more than her, my sisters, who he hasn't seen since they were very little. But does happiness have to be measured in absolutes?"

Colleen thought about this. "I don't know."

"I don't know either, but what I think," Noah said, drawing her closer, pulling her into his warmth, where she was safe; where she'd disappear, if she could. "What I think is that we can't have happiness unless we've seen and felt what the opposite is like. And I don't think happiness is the absence of pain, either. I think it's finding the places where the light comes in, despite the pain. It's about moments." He wrapped their tangled hands behind her back and gazed down at her. "Like this one."

"Moments," she repeated. She let her eyes lock on his, despite the almost magnetic pull to look away; to break the intensity. To retreat to a place where her heart was safe.

"Moments," he said again. "Like the moment when we see your mother and my father realize their children are happy. Like the moment where you'll hold Olivia for the first time, or your brother's new son, who will enter the world any day now. When you meet my dad, and I meet your mom, and New Orleans stops feeling like a place where a guy like me and a girl like you could never have found one another."

"I could love you anywhere, Noah," Colleen protested. Another, less welcome, thought also jumped into her head: *But will he love me when he knows what I can do?*

"Now," he said softly. "But we don't need to paint the past with a different brush, Colleen. Our worlds intersected here, not there. But now we can take that same bridge home."

Home. There was that word again. And now, as she let herself disappear into the warmth and safety of real love, she understood that home wasn't a place at all.

Charles had to remind himself to breathe as he watched the French nymph search for the right words in English to describe her background.

"Don't struggle too hard," Cordelia barked. "My son needs to speak English. Do you?"

Lisette looked stricken by the comment. Charles resisted the powerful urge to kneel in front of her and assure her that even if his son grew up speaking perfect French, it would be okay. Just fine.

"I speak English," she protested. Her tiny mouth, red as a cherry, turned into a pout. "Your son will speak English."

"Not very good English, if he learns it from you."

"Cordelia," Charles warned. He turned to the beautiful girl and tried to pretend he was not blinded by her presence, in every way. "Lisette, we appreciate you coming here and helping us."

"We're paying her, darling," Cordelia said, and he felt her eyes roll at his side. "She's not running a charity."

"I love children," Lisette insisted. She tangled her hands together in her lap. Her blond hair hung limply past her face as if she could hide there. She was a bundle of nerves. "I raise my sisters. I wish to have many children of my own."

"If I want broken English, I'll visit a convenience store in New Orleans," Cordelia quipped. "We have very little time before our son is born. Do we need to pay for English lessons?"

"That's not necessary at all," Charles said and realized he hadn't stopped smiling since the girl walked in. Not once. Not even for a moment. His cheeks hurt. "Right, Lisette?"

"I do not believe necessary," she replied.

"I don't want our son in a special needs school," Cordelia said.

"I'll work with her."

"You'll what?"

Charles tuned out his wife and leaned in. The connection between him and Lisette was electric. How did Cordelia not feel it? How did the electricity in the house not flicker, even once? "I'll just spend whatever time is needed to let you practice, so you can perfect it."

"You do that for me?"

"I see your reputation has not made it to the servant quarters of the illiterate French," Cordelia murmured. "Child, how old are you?"

"Sixteen, ma'am. Seventeen in fall."

"Still a baby, though legal enough for Charles, I suppose. Darling, where *do* you draw the line?"

Charles ignored her. "Lisette, my mother didn't speak very good English when she came here, and she learned from watching television and reading books. Now, she speaks it so well you'd never know she was raised speaking Irish."

"What is it with you and your brother, and immigrants, anyway?" Cordelia asked. "You both get hard over foreign pity cases."

"Your mother is very nice. She get me this job," Lisette said.

"She knows what it's like to be in your shoes."

"Charles, your mother fucked a rich widower whose wife wasn't even fresh in her *grave*, and then married him like she was doing *him* the favor."

"Cordelia's pregnancy hormones are turning her into a bitch," Charles explained, smile still beaming, right at Lisette, only for Lisette. "Forgive her."

"My husband thinks with his dick, Lisette, you should know."

Lisette's wide, curious eyes passed between the couple.

"I think you need a nap, darling," he said, without breaking his transfixed gaze on the young nanny.

"At least take her to the bedroom," Cordelia said as she leaned back to push herself up off the chaise. "People sit on these couches."

. . .

"I DON'T THINK MRS. DESCHANEL LIKES ME," LISETTE said when Cordelia was gone.

"She doesn't like anyone, Lisette. Should I call you Lisette? Do you have a nickname?"

"My mother calls me Lis. You can, if you like."

Charles' smile widened. "I do like."

The young woman shuffled in her seat. She was uncomfortable here. Maybe even rethinking this assignment.

Charles took a risk and leaned in. He reached for her hands and was quicker than she was, too quick for her to recoil. They were tiny, like a porcelain doll. *She* was like a doll, with her unmarred baby flesh and innocent doe eyes. "Don't listen to Cordelia. She's like that with me, too. I don't think she was held much as a baby." He cleared his throat. "I'll always be here, Lis. You don't need to worry about Cordelia, or anyone else, just me. You have a problem, you come to me." He ran his thumb over the soft, smooth flesh covering the top of her delicate hands. "Or for anything. Doesn't have to be bad."

Her face flushed. "*Merci*, Mr. Deschanel." She winced. "I mean, thank you."

"Charles," he corrected. He pressed one, then both of her hands to his lips. "And you can speak whatever language you like, Lis."

COLIN LAUGHED SO HARD HE HAD TO COVER HIS MOUTH to avoid spitting out his beer.

"In love," he repeated, snorting to clear his nose of rogue hops. "And how many times is this now, Huck?"

For real? Just once. "I know, I know."

"You just met her!"

"I know!"

"And she's... she's sixteen."

"She'll be seventeen very soon."

"Charles August Deschanel."

"I *know.*"

"And you're married."

"To a hellbeast."

Colin shook his head. He removed the napkin from his lap—only Colin would put a napkin in his lap to drink beer—and dabbed at first his mouth and then eyes. "Only you, Charles. Only you."

Charles narrowed his eyes. "You think I'm joking."

Colin's head shook as he laughed. "I know you're not joking. You never are. Not when it's about women."

"I can't tell if you're judging me, or happy for me."

"Does it matter?"

"Yeah. It does."

Colin set his napkin aside, neatly folded. "Look, I know you think I'm a traditionalist."

Charles pursed his lips. "Think?"

"Okay." Colin raised his hands in surrender. His eyes glinted with a touch of mischief from behind his glasses, which were new. "I *am* a traditionalist. But I've *met* your wife, Charles. I understand why you might feel inclined to... stray."

"It's just us here. You can call that bitch a hellbeast if you want."

"I'd prefer not to disparage women, even that one, if it's all the same to you."

Charles raised both hands.

"But I've watched you fall in love a hundred times over the years. You meet a girl in the bar, tell me this is the one, take her home, and then tomorrow it's another girl. I don't know if you've ever really been in love, but it's not fireworks and passion, it's something deeper. It's what remains when those things are gone, and you realize she's your best friend and even without the fireworks you still want to be around her."

Delusions are powerful, Colin. "This is different."

"How?"

I haven't thought of Catherine even once when I was with Lisette. "It just is."

"I see." Colin nodded. "What does Cordelia think?"

"She knows who she married. Just as I know who I did."

"What happens, Charles," Colin said after a careful pause, "when you realize she's no different than the others, and she's still there, raising your son?"

"She *is* different," Charles said, growing frustrated, because if he couldn't explain it to Colin, how could he be so sure of what he *felt* so sure of?

Colin raised his glass with a smile, but his eyes belied a long-suffering sadness, one he reserved for times just like this one, with his best friend. "Then I wish you the best, Huck. You know I've only ever wanted you to be happy."

I was, once.

And then I wasn't.

But that doesn't mean I can't be.

SUMMER 1975

VACHERIE, LOUISIANA
NEW ORLEANS, LOUISIANA
EDINBURGH, SCOTLAND

CHAPTER 6

Crazy on You

Cordelia had left a note. *Gone to final appointment.* No *Love, Cordelia*. No signs of affection. Just a no-nonsense series of words, and the subtext that required no further interpretation. Gone to final appointment, *alone.*

Charles balled the note in his fist and threw it across the room. He couldn't keep up with the bitch's moods at all. For months, she'd allowed him to play a role in his son's development, and now, she'd taken this away, as quickly as she'd given it. She didn't have the imagination for playing games, so the only conclusion he could draw was cruelty.

She claimed not to care about his roving eye, and this was probably true for the most part, but that was before Lisette. Before his desires lived under the same roof as their façade of a family. Cordelia had no mind for jealousy, but there was an especial brand of effrontery involved in waving your mistress under your wife's nose.

Charles had every intention of making the young, supple Lisette Duchene his mistress.

Because she wasn't Cordelia.

More to the point, she wasn't Cat.

As he turned away, he caught someone pick the wad of paper off the floor. Lisette looked at it with a strange, almost guilty expression, then held it out.

"Just toss it," Charles said, but he had the sudden, powerful urge to take the paper between his teeth, and pass it to her, mouth to mouth, as he ravaged her on the secretary the note had been scribbled on.

Now who's the vengeful bitch?

"You dropped it?"

"I threw it."

"You mean to throw?"

"I meant it and then some."

Lisette seemed reluctant. She held it out like a bloody carcass and made her way to the kitchen.

"Do you have everything you need?"

Lisette turned. "*Monsieur*?"

"Here, I mean, Lis. Do you have what you need?"

"This house is so beautiful. How could I not have what I need?"

"Yes, but are you... uh, happy?"

Lisette smiled. "You ask me that every day."

"I promised I'd look after you here."

"I don't need you to protect me, *Monsieur*."

Yes. You do. "You didn't answer."

"No one asks if someone is happy. What use is happy?"

"Did your mother teach you that?" Charles felt, for a moment, as if he was sparring with his own mother, who had always given happiness a backseat to anything practical. You didn't need to like what you ate, it only needed to sustain you. Who cared if you were too cold, or too hot, at least you had a roof over your head. Lisette's mother and Irish Colleen were cut from the same cloth.

"My mother teach me to first take care of me and my own. Knowing my family is fed and safe is happiness."

"That's surviving, Lis. Not happiness."

"Does not each person get to define their own happiness?"

Charles frowned. The question was fair, but it confounded him. If happiness was a moving target on a sliding scale, how could anyone know if they'd hit it? *I* was *happy once. I know that was happiness. And if not, then it was good enough for me.*

"I can't argue that," Charles said. "But you still haven't answered my question."

"Am I happy?"

"Yes."

Lisette licked her luscious cherry lips and then ran her teeth over the bottom one. "I have you, Monsieur. You see to my needs, even ones I do not know I have."

Oh, yes. You have me all right.

COLLEEN THRUST HER HIPS UPWARD AND USED THE momentum of Noah's delighted surprise to roll them in one deft move, positioning herself on top of him, where she was in control.

Oh, how Colleen had always craved control in all things. All things except sex, which she'd never understood beyond the physiological response—Philip—or the societal expectation—Rory. She'd allowed both men to lead her in the direction they felt best, assuming the defect was hers. What else could explain it, when she'd loved Rory and desired Philip? Two sides of the sexual coin, and she'd experienced both, but neither left her fulfilled.

With Noah, that last missing piece of herself snapped into place and locked there, refusing to budge. She didn't only love him. She needed him. She craved him. She needed to crave him, and for him to crave her, and, at last, her control of this synched with every other part of her and she was whole.

Noah's head rolled back against the pillow as she commanded her body, moving over him in slow, deliberate strides. He was ready to come. Had been ready, but her own climb to climax heightened at the sight of her undoing his resolve... at drawing every last tendril of orgasm from him and demanding it sit, waiting, patiently, until she decided it was time.

Colleen spread his sweaty hair off his brow and kissed the spot where it had clung. *I love you so much it terrifies me.* "Come for me," she purred, and he did.

CHARLES FOUND LISETTE LATER THAT AFTERNOON, making her bed. Cordelia hadn't come home yet from her appointment and hadn't called to say she'd be delayed. He had no idea where she was and ordinarily wouldn't especially care, except she was giving birth to his son any day.

He'd decided to call one of his contacts to have her tracked, when Lisette appeared in his peripheral. For such a large house, she had a way of being where he was, just when he began to miss her.

"Hey, you don't have to do that."

She looked up, surprised. "Do what?"

"You know, clean. We have a staff for that."

Lisette chuckled to herself and continued spreading the comforter across the top of the sheets. "I didn't come here to be spoiled, *Monsieur.*"

None of the girls, and later women, he'd been raised around acted this way. None of them could have pulled off that wide-eyed innocence; that naivete about the way the world was supposed to work. She was one step away from a maid's uniform, asking to be spanked with a feather duster.

But she really *was* from another world. One where the thought of anyone doing for you was so foreign it was offensive. What did she think of him, then? Of a man who was king and center of that world?

Maybe all the coquetry was part of the job for her.

"I'm curious, Lisette," he said. "What did you come here to do? Now, I don't mean the money. Everyone who works, works because they need money for something. What is that something, for you?"

Lisette paused for the most fleeting moment before smoothing the comforter. She kept herself focused on the task at hand, never looking up. "A girl like me does not have many choices. My mother marry poor man and lived poor life." She tilted her head to the side. Some of her blond hair spilled out of the tie at her neck. "I don't need much. Only that my children, when I have them, don't know how it feels to go to bed hungry." She waved her hand around the room with a hard smile. "What's all this, to someone like me? A dream? It's no dream of mine. People, they think dreams are dangerous. My people think that. I say it is only dangerous to dream so big you forget why you had dreams to begin with."

Charles had no acceptable answer for her, and he was too busy falling in love to think of how to respond. It was no wonder he'd never met a woman he wanted to be with more than once or twice, because the women in his circle never dreamed of anything. What was there to dream of, when you had everything? Catherine was a dreamer, because she knew hardship and knew the value of wishing for better. But Catherine dreamed too big. She always had, and she dreamed so big she forgot why she had dreams to begin with.

"I can't imagine what you must think of me, Lis," he said. "Living like this."

She shrugged. "You have all this, but it doesn't mean you have everything."

"What am I missing?" Would she travel down the path he was heading?

But she only smiled. Her blue eyes twinkled as she watched him, patient but distant. "It is not for me to say, *Monsieur.*"

Colleen danced around the sides of Noah as she dropped herbs and spices into the dish he was cooking, fancying herself a bona fide sous chef. Or even better, playing wife to a husband. She imagined them five years from now, children running around the hearth as they sipped their favorite wine together. She saw them twenty years in the future, drinking that same wine as they both celebrated, and lamented, their empty nest.

"Whoa, whoa, whoa!" he cried and tore the cayenne from her hands. "Are you trying to turn us into an incendiary device?"

Colleen gasped at the sea of orangish red floating atop the roux. "Oh no."

"Well, we *are* from New Orleans," he said and grabbed one more pinch from the open can in her hand. "Unless our time in the Highlands has turned us into wimps."

"You, maybe."

"I'm the goalpost for masculinity."

"Too bad the real tough ones are the women."

"True," he said as he stirred. "I think I'd rather have sons than daughters, though. They're less complicated."

Colleen laughed. "But your daughters will run the world someday."

"Also true."

Children. They'd joked about this from time to time, in light-hearted ways ascribing their best and worst characteristics to their future nonexistent offspring. But Noah had been making these jokes more frequently now, and she couldn't help but wonder if he was hedging closer to a serious conversation on the topic.

"You've thought about this a lot," she ventured. "Having children?"

Noah shrugged and did a spin move around her as he reached for the burner. "I could take or leave having children, to be perfectly honest. My childhood wasn't exactly normal. I'm not sure what normal is supposed to look like."

"I can relate to that."

Noah laughed. "The Goddess of the Garden District, ladies and gentleman."

"Why do you do that?"

"What?"

"Assume being wealthy means my life was good?"

Noah set the spoon on the rest. "I don't know," he admitted. "Because, growing up without money I suppose I had an unhealthy view of how well it would have solved our problems."

"It solved some," she agreed. "But it created others. And the worst of our problems had nothing to *do* with money. Some of us, like Augustus, like me, have tried to rise above it and be our own people. I came *here* because I didn't want doors to open because of who I was. I wanted to earn my way. And I'm not naïve enough to believe having money hasn't helped me, or won't help me, but growing up a Deschanel was its own special brand of dysfunctional. Trust me."

Noah kissed her cheek. "Then tell me."

I wish I could tell you everything. I don't know how. "Maybe *after* you meet my family, so you don't change your mind about marrying me."

"Never."

"Never say never."

"Are you excited to go home? Sometimes you seem like you're dreading it."

Colleen laughed. "I am dreading it! But I want them to know you, Noah." She turned toward him and took both his hands in hers. "I'm afraid of what they'll think. Not of you, but me. I know they'll love you. My mother will fall all over herself to charm you, because you'll remind her of her own world."

"Then what? Is it the difference in... who we are?"

Colleen shook her head before he could let that fear sink in too deep and take hold. "Augustus married a woman who had nothing but the clothes on her back. They won't care about that. It's more that I worry they'll question my judgment in falling for someone and agreeing to marry them after a long weekend. I know, *I know*, what I am feeling is real, no question. But I've created this image of myself as being reasonable and thoughtful in everything I do, and how I feel about you is a new side of me. One they won't recognize."

Noah finished stirring and tossed the spoon aside. He pulled her in. His warmth sent chills all through her. "I love this side of you. I love *every* side of you."

"You haven't seen all sides of me."

"I already know I'll love them." He kissed her. "I'm not worried about it, Colleen. When you love someone this much, it's not about fearing the dark sides. It's about being safe to show them. Whatever I don't know about you, I'm not scared now, and I won't be when you sprout three heads and come into your final form, either."

Colleen smiled into his kiss. "Four heads."

"Well, *four* might be one too many."

She saw them forty years from now, as their grandkids played in the yard of the house they'd built from their memories of Scotland. Their final place to enjoy retirement.

Marriage only seemed impractical until you met the man you saw yourself growing old with.

CHAPTER 7

Try, Try Again

Ekatherina ended up in the hospital again, right as Cordelia was admitted for delivery. Early, just as she predicted.

Augustus and Charles massed together at roughly the center point between the rooms of the two women. They'd both been booted from the respective suites by their wives, one from anger, the other, cruelty. The men in the hall were responsible for landing them in their respective predicaments and were unwelcome.

"I didn't know she could be so angry." Augustus crossed his arms. "She was always so *quiet* in the office, and even when I took her to Maine..." He glanced repeatedly down the hall, hoping to see a nurse gesturing to him to return. "She loathes my presence, and I don't know what I did to deserve it. I'm at a loss. It defies logic."

"My son is being born and this wench knows right where to stick the knife and turn," Charles grumbled. He wouldn't stop moving. The small circle he cut with his pacing screeched with the sharp angles created by his sneakers. The sound was met with dirty looks by passersby. "I knew all that nice crap she was pulling was a ruse to get me to lower my guard, so she could fuck me right in the ass with her vengeance."

"She may even hate me," Augustus said. "I can't wrap my head around it."

"If I really wanted to be in that room, there's not a fucking thing that bitch could do to stop me."

"She blames me for her sister. What else could I do? Should I fly to New York and strongarm the immigration office?"

"Won't she be shocked when she looks down through her legs expecting to see my boy and she sees my merciless fucking face. Surprise, bitch."

"I don't know what I'm supposed to do. I always know what to do. I'm not sure I can fix this."

"Maybe I'll go in there and play doctor and deliver him myself. Double surprise, bitch."

The brothers projected their fears into words, not really talking to each other, or even at each other. They were hardly aware of one another, except in the subtle comfort they drew from proximity.

If Augustus was going to be standing in this hospital with anyone, he was glad it was Charles.

"Mr. Deschanel?"

Both brothers whipped their heads at the sound of their name.

"Augustus," the doctor corrected.

Augustus exchanged a wary look with his brother. Charles shook his head and went back to pacing.

"She's waking up now," the doctor explained. He set her chart in the holder. "The sedative we gave her was mild. We're very limited in our options when a woman is pregnant."

"Of course." Augustus stuffed his sweaty hands in his trouser pockets. "Did she ask for me?"

"No, but you did request we notify you when she wakes," the doctor answered. His nervous look back toward Ekatherina's room betrayed what he didn't say. "Please be aware, Mr. Deschanel, it is *very* important that we keep your wife calm. I believe your O.B. already discussed the risks her stress could pose to the health of both her and your unborn child."

"Yes."

He tapped his pen against his thigh, thinking. With a look suggesting he might regret saying it, he added, "She asked me not to tell you she was awake. Now, I'm not in the business of marital counseling, and what's happened between you two is between you two. It's none of mine whether you've got bad blood in the marriage. I can't tell a husband to stay out of his wife's room, and I won't. But... consider treading carefully."

Augustus' cheeks burned as it slowly dawned on him what the doctor was implying. "Doctor, that's *not* what's happening here. My wife has suffered a loss, and she's reacting to *that*. She thinks there's more I could have done to bring her sister here, where she could have received treatment that might have saved her life. She blames me. That's all."

The doctor held up his hands. "You don't owe me an explanation, Augustus. Not the first time I've turned a blind eye, and won't be the last. But don't make me regret it."

Augustus stepped closer. He lowered his voice. "Doctor, I am *not* abusing my wife, and I detest the insinuation."

The doctor smiled knowingly, nodding. "Of course. We never had this conversation."

Augustus was horrified. Had this doctor really allowed the abuse of women to be glossed over, out of some archaic notion of fraternity?

He grabbed the doctor's arm as he started to walk away. He didn't know what he was doing. Was he really going to do this? Here? Now? He'd never done this so impulsively, without thought, without weighing out the risks.

Augustus burned his eyes into the doctor's. He pressed all his focus into one channel. "You will stop protecting terrible men. Your priority from now on is ensuring the safety of the women who trust you with their health. In fact, I think you're going to donate thirty percent of this year's salary to an organization that provides relief for battered woman. Next year, too, and hell, why not the year after? Sound good?"

"Sounds good," the doctor replied, dazed.

"Sounds like the least you can do," Augustus countered and left the doctor in the hallway, drawing from his well of strength as he stepped through the door of Ekatherina's room.

Colin came upon Charles as he was yelling at a pack of cowering nurses. An ashy cigarette flailed around in one hand while the other pointed with escalating vigor.

"Colin! Finally, someone who knows what the *fuck* is going on here. Can you please explain to these workers whose salaries I help pay that I have *every goddamn right* to be in the room when my own flesh and blood comes into this world?"

"Charles. Can we talk?"

"Now? Really? Does this look like a good time for a little chitty chat?"

Colin smiled placatingly at the shell-shocked nurses. "Ladies, will you excuse us?"

"No, they won't *fucking* excuse us, not until they let me into that goddamn room."

"Sorry," Colin said over his head and all but dragged him to a small seating area in the corner of the ward. "What's gotten into you?"

"Stop apologizing for me. That was bullshit, the way you acted like I was the bad guy."

Colin smelled at the air and curled his nose in disgust. "You've been drinking. Today of all days."

"What better reason is there on this entire planet than the birth of my first son?"

"One could argue the birth of one's son is a more compelling reason *not* to drink, for once in your life. Tell me you're not high, too."

Charles sniffed; it was a phantom reaction, now second nature. He wished he were high, but he'd forgotten his stash at Ophélie, and he wasn't leaving until these incompetents let him into the birthing suite.

"Since you're here," Charles answered. He pointed his cigarette toward the nurse's station, gesturing wildly. "Help me deal with this bullshit."

"I can try," Colin said. His eyes darted around. He was embarrassed, the poor baby. Charles wanted to hurl him like a bowling ball, right into the gaggle of useless women who knew only how to say no, or I'm sorry.

"Steeee-rike!" Charles cried out. He sniffed. God, what a foolish thing to forget at home. He wondered if he could score off someone here. If anyone was the ideal consumer for some high quality coke, it was those high-strung-bloated-salary motherfuckers running around all day and night. If every doc on this staff wasn't as keyed up as he'd like to be right now, he'd eat his hat.

"What are you on about now?"

"I'm an excellent bowler."

"You're... what?" Colin craned his neck down both ends of the hallway. Charles mimed doing the same with a slack-jawed expression and a few ridiculous slurs to match.

"Why are you even here?" Charles asked, as it occurred to him he hadn't called his friend nor was there any obvious reason for him to be at the hospital, other than to annoy him and serve as chief judge.

"I'm *here* because as soon as your son is born, I need you to sign paperwork naming him as your heir."

Charles threw his head back and laughed. He slapped the wall, cackling as if he'd been privy to the funniest joke in the world. His humor died away as Colin's expression evolved to be gradually more and more annoyed.

Charles cleared his throat. "That can't wait?"

"Technically, legally, it can. Absolutely," Colin replied. Everything about him changed when he morphed into Lawyer Colin. The way he held himself, his voice, his choice of words. "But your ancestors had a stipulation—you might consider it ceremonial—that the honor be granted at the moment of birth."

"Ce*re*mon*ial*," Charles parroted. He enunciated each syllable with escalating flair.

"Yes, it seems that men who have billions to hand down possess the prerogative of doing so with pomp and circumstance."

"Will there be a band, Colin? Tell me you've booked the Stones."

"No, Charles. There will not be a band."

The heat from the overhead lights was overwhelming. Charles broke out in a sudden sweat at the realization, and from then on it was all he could think of. He ran his hands around the exposed areas of his flesh in no particular pattern.

But then as quick as the onset of heat had descended, he began shivering. Full body shakes, and a chill to the depth of his bones.

Around him, the hospital went about their work as if the room had not turned from fire to ice.

"You're nervous," Colin said. He draped a tentative arm over Charles' shoulder, not quite resting it against his humming flesh. "Of course you are. I was a mess when Oz was born. To tell you the truth, I still am."

"I don't know what the fuck is wrong with this place, but this shit is Biblical. Like my wedding day."

"What is?" Colin's head shuddered as he thought better of the question. "I have an idea. It could be hours before Cordelia delivers, so why don't we get a coffee?"

"No, fuck coffee."

"Right." Colin dropped his arm and again scanned the hospital. What the hell was he looking at? "How about we find Augustus? He's dealing with a lot of stress, too. He could use the company."

"He's in with that Russian."

"Ekatherina."

"She doesn't get a name until she starts respecting my brother."

"Right."

"Stop saying that."

"What?"

"Right. Stop saying *right,* like I'm some fucking madman you can't hold a conversation with."

Colin cocked his head to say, *well...*

"Did you come here to help, or to flaunt your perfection in my face?"

"I told you why I'm here," Colin said. "We could've sent my dad. He's probably the more appropriate person to handle this, since he's lead on the Deschanel account, and he went through this once before, when you were born. But I said I wanted to come, because I thought you could use a friend, Huck. I know you're scared, because this is scary. And Cordelia, well, she doesn't make it easy. I get that."

"Fucking understatement."

"But," Colin went on, "once your son is born, you'll forget about her. You'll forget about your ire toward the nurses, and how you're feeling right now. It will all fall away, and you'll be completely and totally in awe of the new life that's half you, and all Deschanel. He's your heir, but he's also your *son*, and there's nothing else in the world that feels more like magic than that. Not even to someone like you, who grew up around the real deal."

Charles fought the urge to cry. He didn't know where it had come from. He never cried, unless he was too high to know what the fuck was happening. Tears were pointless, but they were also scary and wild and a symptom of a bigger problem, which was a lack of control. There was no greater sin than letting anything sneak by that he didn't approve.

"I hate her." Charles' voice dropped low. He sniffed, this time from something other than the phantom cocaine. "I really, really hate her. I've tried to like her, Colin. I know you think half of what I say is full of shit, but I have *tried.* I've tried harder to like Cordelia than I tried in all the wasted years of college. She's not good. And I *am* afraid, but my fear is bigger than these bullshit nurses and their useless words."

Colin stopped his nervous, judgmental shuffling and listened.

"I'm afraid she'll be a terrible mother, and that I won't be good enough to make up for it." Charles crossed his arms and turned completely away when the tears spilled. He gritted his teeth, cussing himself out in his head. This was unacceptable. Complete and utter bullshit. He had to work himself back to the anger, because anger was better. He knew what the fuck *that* meant.

Colin's perpetual smugness disappeared. The change was so absolute that Charles felt it, even though he couldn't see his friend's face. Colin sidled up to Charles, but seemed to understand not to come close enough to witness the unforgivable lapse in emotion. "Terrible parents don't worry about things like this," he said, approaching his words with obvious care. "You've had your share of sins, but none of it will matter by the time today is over. None of it, Huck. Because the Charles Deschanel of yesterday is not the man you are right now. When you hold your son, you'll transform into someone so different from who you are in this very second that you wouldn't believe me if I described him." He reached out and squeezed Charles' arm. "You can't decide who Cordelia will be. But you will be the father your son needs, and Catherine and I will step in and help wherever you need it. Your sisters will step in and show him their own nurturing. You won't be able to keep Irish Colleen away."

Charles sniffed. Laughed.

"He won't want for love. Not in this lifetime."

Charles turned and without lifting his head, he pressed his face into Colin's face, allowing this very temporary lapse into vulnerability, with one of the few men who knew him enough to give him such reassurances.

"YOU LIE TO ME!"

Augustus was helpless against the ire. He dared not say anything to further incite her, but he hadn't said anything to bring her wrath upon him when he walked in, either. He was frozen by his fear of the irrational. Anything he said could make this worse. He doubted anything would make it better.

"Ekatherina, I never lied to you. I've probably failed you in other ways, but I've always been very honest with you about the roadblocks I've faced trying to get your family here."

She whipped her face to the side, away, an active denial of him and his words. "You say you can help. You convince me to *marry* you, and I do, for this!"

Augustus winced. She was angry and grieving her loss. She clearly didn't mean it.

It still stung.

"I've tried everything I know. I've offered money, and more money. I've used my influence. The one thing I can't change is the political climate." Augustus pulled his seat close to her and tried to ignore her instinctual recoil. Was this, here, now, the truer reflection of her feelings for him? Now that his usefulness was spoiled, was her love, also? Or was this really only grief talking?

"I care nothing for politic, *husband.*" This last was said with such acrimony that Augustus' stomach clenched into a tight knot.

"I know you don't," he said, attempting to come across as gentle and soothing. Neither were characteristics that were very natural for him, and he worried this was obvious enough to make things even worse than they were. He didn't know what worse looked like. He didn't want to. "But I'm learning the hard way that even my best has limitations."

"Your *best* is nothing. It's no use to me. It kill my sister!"

Augustus sighed inwardly. Nothing he said would get through to her, because she wasn't in the frame of mind to be rational. She'd taken one word and twisted it into something vile, and she'd keep doing it. There would be no end to his faults.

Later, he would evaluate this. Not simply this conversation or the few preceding it, but his entire courtship and marriage. Somewhere, his judgment had failed him. Perhaps several somewheres. He could spend time convincing himself her words were born of emotion, or he could accept that at no point in their relationship had their love been two-sided. Even when she folded herself into his arms in Maine, he suspected her behavior to be the culmination of her feelings for another. And could she be blamed, truly? He'd known all along he was not the marrying type. He'd loved and pursued her anyway. Insanity was going against your better judgment and then having the gall to be surprised when it ended up exactly as it should have.

Later, remember? Unless you want to do this now, when she's wild with hatred for you? Is this helping?

"I love you," he blurted. The words came from somewhere within him, but it was a place he recognized no better than the side of him who had forsaken himself for the love that led him to this very moment.

"*Hmph.*" The heart rate beeps on her monitor blipped faster and more frequently every time she spoke. Over time, they'd gradually increased, and he'd watched this with apprehension. Any higher, and it would trigger an alarm. "Love. You say you love me. You say you do anything for me. You don't know anything."

"I'm so sorry about Anasofiya," he hazarded. "I would have moved the world to get her here. To get all of them here."

"My world is destroyed. It is nothing now. You destroy it."

"I loved you enough to forget who I was and become someone you could love, too."

"You don't know love. You know power. You know to take what you want because you never lived like I live. You are spoiled and eat from silver and that is not love. You use love. You don't know it."

I never wanted any of it. I tried to walk away from my name and everything it stood for. I focused on myself, on... Maddy. On my business. On Evangeline. On everything except all those things you would persecute me for.

But then, you.

"I can't deny who I am, Ekatherina," Augustus said. He needed to leave. She didn't want him here, and it hurt more than he could manage to hear her say the words, when on some level he knew she meant them. He reached for her, to touch her, but thought better of it. Instead, he went to the door. He lingered long enough to add, "But you're wrong about my love. I've never given it freely, or easily. Until you, I didn't know I could."

. . .

Colin was a force. He might have treated Charles like a toddler in need of extreme babysitting when he'd arrived at the hospital, but as soon as the announcement of Cordelia's safe delivery was made, he turned into another man entirely. He commanded that the wing be cleared of all but essential personnel. He informed—didn't ask, but directed—the doctor that he was to bring the baby to a private room for Charles to see him and hold him, once Cordelia had held him first.

Before the doctor could act on the orders, a flurry of activity drew their attention to Cordelia's room. Two other doctors rushed in, and it all happened very fast. One minute she was resting quietly, and the next, she was being wheeled to surgery, for reasons no one paused to explain.

"What's happening? What's going on?" Charles asked every last person who ran by him, but he received only one word in response, from a harried nurse taking up the rear: *bleeding*.

"Charles," Colin said to bring him back to the moment. "I'll stay on top of Cordelia's situation. Right now, you should be with your son."

"My son," Charles whispered as he gaped down the hall where his wife had just been wheeled away. He needed to ground himself. To remember what was important. "Yes, my son. My son! Where is he?"

A nurse appeared, smiling. "Come with me, Mr. Deschanel."

Colin nodded to follow her. "I'll deal with this. Go."

Charles wandered several paces behind the nurse. Everything around him had faded to a blur, like the dream sequence of a movie. Faded, hazy, lighter.

He entered the room he'd watched the nurse disappear into. The effect of his daze intensified and for years after he would swear that he'd seen a halo of heavenly light appear around the woman holding his son.

Her smile was warm and beckoning. "You ready to meet your son, Mr. Deschanel?"

Charles accepted the tiny bundle. He was daunted with how

light the weight was and how little it pushed at his arms, but at the same time, how *heavy* he felt.

A wrinkled, reddish face peeked out from the swath of blanket. Eyes closed, mouth twisted as the wee one adjusted to his new reality.

His son.

"Have you and your wife picked out a name?"

Charles didn't think he could speak, but these were the words he'd been waiting to say for months, and he wouldn't miss his first chance to say them aloud.

Looking down at the best thing he'd ever done, Charles said, "Nicolas Charles Deschanel."

COLIN GAVE CHARLES THE NEWS AS HE WATCHED, IN awe, as Nicolas slept.

He would murder Cordelia later, but the Charles sitting in the nursery next to his newborn son was a changed man.

"Do you understand what this means?"

"Yes, Colin," Charles said, measuring his voice in sweet, dulcet tones. If Cordelia's wickedness disturbed Nicolas for even a second, it would be an unforgivable sin. "It means she can't have more kids unless that kid is Jesus."

Colin exhaled into his lap. He'd folded himself over his knees, hands pressed together. "I don't know how she managed it. The scene. The drama. I really thought something was wrong with her."

"Something *is* wrong with her," Charles said sweetly as Nicolas' sleeping hand tried to grab the finger he'd used to tickle his palm. "She's a psychopath. I've told you that all along."

"Emergency hysterectomy." Colin mulled the words, as if he might suddenly understand the mind of someone as soulless as Cordelia Hendrickson. "How did she convince the doctor to perform such a procedure?"

"She just sold her shares in her father's failing company. She had more than enough to buy off these incompetents." Charles didn't want to think about this just now. He wanted to go to wherever Nicolas' sweet baby imagination had taken him. Wanted to jump cotton candy fences on their matching ponies as the pink sun rained colorful sprinkles.

"But *why*?"

"Why do pigs roll around in their own shit? Because they like it, Colin. She likes being this way. It's probably the only damn thing she likes."

"Doesn't it negate the whole value of marrying you?"

"She gave me a son," Charles said. "A legitimate son, not a child born from a woman we paid off, somewhere in another state."

"You don't want other kids?"

Charles leaned into the crib and blew soft kisses against Nicolas' cheeks. Nicolas wiggled in his tiny pajamas in response.

"Huck, I'm sorry... I don't know what I was thinking, talking to you about this now."

Charles plucked at Nicolas' tiny toes. "Don't be. It gives me a reason to throw her ass out onto the street without feeling the least bit of remorse."

"I'm really *so* sorry. I can't believe she would do this... and today, of all days. The sight of her own son inspired her to do *this.*"

"I know this is hard for someone of your moral caliber to understand," Charles said. "But women like Cordelia exist. Monsters are real, Colin. They're all around us." He tucked the blanket around his son and turned around to face his friend. "But you know who does want kids? A whole fucking lot of them, according to her."

Colin looked confused.

Charles grinned. "Lisette."

"You can't be... you are. You're *serious.*"

Charles redirected his attention back to his son, where his only happiness lived now. "We'll talk later."

CHAPTER 8

The Witch

The anticipation of their impending trip home was nearing conclusion. In just one week, Colleen and Noah would be on a plane back to New Orleans, and their news, public.

Her usual optimism had been replaced by an uncomfortable sullenness, one Noah picked up on. He didn't ask her about it. Instead, he found ways to bring her back to herself without saying a thing.

"Let's go to Skye," he whispered to Colleen one afternoon, as she lost herself in an anatomy textbook.

She snapped the tome closed and smiled. "You always have the best ideas."

THE WORLD WAS A BLANKET OF VIOLET HEATHER. RAIN showered upon the earth, inch after inch, bringing summer floods and havocked roads. Colleen wrung her hands in anxiousness, thinking of Madeline. Never again would riding in a car feel the same to her, and Maddy would always be front of mind whenever the roads felt dangerous.

Noah pressed his hand against her knee, insisting they could turn around, that Skye would be there at the end of summer. He didn't mention Maddy, but he knew about her fears, and their connection to her own tragedy.

Colleen's objective to serve her family did not include cowardice, though. Madeline's tragic death had been a painful occurrence, not a tether, preventing her from living her life. If Noah's presence had taught her anything, it was the need to open her eyes. Her horizons need not be narrow or fearful.

Outside of Glasgow, the rain turned to downpour. Noah pulled off the road at a rest stop to wait for the worst to pass. They huddled together in the car, rubbing their hands over the heater vents.

"New Orleans doesn't sound so bad right now, eh?" he joked.

"Just our luck, we'll bring the rain there."

When the rain didn't subside, they rented a hotel room on the outskirts of the city. Colleen allowed herself to succumb to her latent grief over her sister, which had been cruelly triggered by the hazardous drive. It snuck up on her, in a tremendous wave, and it was as if Maddy had died just that morning. She'd allowed herself almost no time for grief years earlier, and her sadness now came from that same suppressed well. Noah held her all night as she cried. He never pretended to assure her the sadness would end, only that he would love her through it. That he would love her through anything.

Nor did he ask again if she wanted to turn back.

The sun broke through the storm the next morning. Hopeful, they journeyed on, making it as far as Glencoe before the clouds turned dark and the heavens again rained down. Narrow Highland roads were flooded from two days of heavy downpour, and Noah slowed the car to a crawl, the Vauxhall gliding more over water than roads.

"This has to be a joke." Noah butted his palm against the steering wheel. "This is insane."

"We need to find another place to stop." Colleen's voice stammered, her panic rising to something she'd never experienced before: a premonition they were headed down a dreadful path.

"I know," Noah replied, jaw clenched. His knuckles, white and unsteady, gripped the wheel. "I can't see a damn thing. If you spot anything, tell me."

All Colleen saw through the storm was the green rise and fall of the glen, and flocks of sheep and Highland cows grazing. The road ahead had disappeared beyond a handful of feet to their front and gentle sloping land on the sides.

"There should be—" was all Colleen got out before the unexpected bend in the road came upon them. The glided, out beyond the safety railing. The sick crash of metal bounced through her skull and blocked out all other sound or sensation.

Silence. The air stilled. Time slowed. Lightheaded, she had the distinct sensation of floating, a feeling unique to her dreams. In the driver's seat, Noah's head tilted back and his mouth gaped, as if screaming, but she heard nothing but the peacefulness of drifting.

Then, with a suddenness immeasurable by time, the serenity in Colleen's mind turned to a thud couched in a blackness that wrapped around her entire world.

Colleen's skull lobbed forward, her neck struggling to support the weight. She had no pain, no fear. Her capable senses helped immediately assess the situation as a result of her shock. She would need to further evaluate the extent of her injuries because she knew the endorphins would only carry her so far. They could be deceptive.

Her vision swam in and out of focus as her head dropped to the right toward Noah, toward... she blinked the blurring away, pleading with her mind to reconcile what her eyes witnessed: a piece of the steel guardrail protruding from Noah's chest.

"No," she whispered, coughing up a spray of blood. "No, no, no, no, no. Noah. Noah!"

Colleen unhinged her seat belt and concentrated on seeing

herself whole and healthy. Cells reproducing, muscles repairing. Bones snapping into place. The pain hit her, but she bit it back, terrified, determined.

She said a silent prayer before maneuvering to face the driver's seat, where Noah lay silent, unmoving.

His chest rose. Her hand against his neck revealed his pulse was slow, but there. She exhaled in relief and didn't think about anything that happened next as she laid hands on him.

With a gasp and a heave, the metal expelled itself from Noah's chest, and he rolled forward against the wheel. Colleen didn't let go. Her hands stayed true even as he jerked and convulsed; red and white blood cells replicated and spread, restoring his life force.

"Oh," Noah said with his first breath when air filled his lungs. "What..." He passed out again.

COLLEEN AWOKE TO FLUORESCENT LIGHTS AGAINST speckled panels, voices around her, the smell of iodine and fresh linens. "Noah." Her voice cracked, but no one heard.

"You're safe, lassie," a man's voice told her, later. "You both are."

No, she thought, her soul twisting, *I've saved our bodies at the expense of our hearts.*

LATER, WHEN COLLEEN WAS ALLOWED TO LEAVE HER room, she ventured to Noah's, only to find him discharged. His bed was made up for the next patient, but the nurse said he'd left her a note.

It said only, *I told you I could love you through anything, but I guess you've made a liar of me. If you'd told me months ago that you'd sold yourself to the devil, we could have saved both of us a lot of heartache. I'll try to recover our deposit, and with that, I'll repay you for the plane ticket. I don't want to owe you anything, or give you any reason to come find me.*

. . .

Colleen didn't remember how she got back to Edinburgh. Someone, some kind soul, she thought. All she remembered was the endless green outside her window, fogged by her grief.

Noah moved fast. All his things were gone from her apartment, and the key slid back under the locked door.

No note this time. He'd already said what he needed to say.

If you'd told me months ago that you'd sold yourself to the devil.

She'd saved his *life*! Yes, she'd lied, but it was for this very reason. Without realizing it, he'd proven to be exactly who she feared he was all along: a man of a big heart, but a very narrow mind.

That night, she called Evangeline and poured her heart out. She left out no details, and when she was done, she fell asleep with the phone still cradled to her tear-stained cheek.

Dearest Colleen,

You haven't been picking up the phone since the night you called me. I understand, though. My heart breaks for you, and it's been on my mind nonstop since we talked. Is there no way to fix this? Surely when he called you a witch, it was a heat-of-the-moment comment, not something he meant with conviction. You saved his life. How can he turn his back on you so callously? Has he really been avoiding you since the accident?

On second thought, maybe he doesn't deserve you. The more I think about his treatment of you, the more my anger boils. You've always been the caretaker for everyone. When Mama is gone, you'll probably be the one who keeps this entire family together. You're selfless and kind and the best sister anyone could ever ask for. And Noah is a fool because you'd make the best wife he could ever hope for, too.

I'm so sad that your trip home was canceled. Not for me, since I wasn't going to be there anyway, but I know you were really excited to meet Olivia and Nicolas. Charles offered to buy me a ticket to come see you, and I think I should. I'm ahead in all my classes, so a few days away in the fall won't hurt. I know you, and you'll throw me out the window, though, if I come without your permission, so please, give me your permission. Okay? I love you. We'll get through this together, same as we always have.

Love, Evie

CHAPTER 9
The Diary

"And in this, I find my strength, wherein my strength had prior been ripped from me with utmost cruelty," Maureen read. "I am born anew."

Olivia cooed. She kicked her chubby legs at the sky in protest of something only she could see, but her eyes were wholly on her mother.

Maureen peppered her soft cheeks with kisses. "You hear that, Liv? Like Hopestill Wolfe, your mommy is born anew." More kisses. "In her love for you."

Her daughter's hair was dark, like hers, and she had a feeling that when Olivia was old enough to run around the house, it would be rich like the color their mahogany furniture must have been, once upon a time. Maureen didn't really know what color Edouard's hair was, because he had so little of it, and what wisps he did have, in his middle-aged-man combover, were faded to gray. For a man not yet fifty, he hadn't aged well at all, and it was one further reminder that, other than the light Olivia brought to their home, they were surrounded invariably by things that were old and dark.

Edouard couldn't resist his daughter, despite what must have been an intense effort to the contrary. He was a man of inflexible routine, but when he'd walk past the room bearing Olivia's cradle, drawn to her high-pitched, delightful sounds, he'd grunt and make the needed adjustments to his morning. Sometimes, Maureen caught him actually *playing* with her, lowering his large hand to tentatively tickle her belly. One time, she'd awoken from her nap to find him holding her! Not with any grace, mind, but with wonder, for certain. She wouldn't go as far as to say love, but there was a glimmer of hope there, that he might one day.

Maureen started drawing the odorous, dusty curtains. The first time she'd tried it on her own, throwing her whole body weight into lugging them sideways, she'd nearly coughed to death from all the dust. She went straight to their head of household and asked that they take care of first cleaning them, and then opening them daily, no later than nine in the morning. Nine, because Edouard left the house at 8:48 sharp. She didn't think he'd approve of the change, but there were ways to avoid that, like closing them again at 5:50 in the evening.

The problem with letting in light was all it then revealed. The staff did well enough cleaning, but you couldn't wipe away scratches and fading from furniture that had never been retouched or refinished. The floors, which had felt old and lovely to Maureen when she first stepped upon them, looked as if someone, or several someones, had been dragged across them, raking their nails in protest.

She wanted the place to be beautiful for her daughter. She wanted Olivia to grow up without a single care in the world, for everything she touched to be gilded. Maureen approached the subject one night over dinner, and Edouard told her that Manfred, their butler, had a complete inventory of all furnishings, their origins, and their value. Anything that was *not* an original piece was fair game. Anything that was, well, she would be mindful never to mention such an effrontery again.

Manfred, with a decrepit, humorless grin, showed her the ledger. He let her read over it, despite knowing quite well what the outcome would be.

"Only *two* things in this house are not originals? Two?"

"If you count the appliances, ten!"

"Are you sure this is right?"

"Are you questioning the efficacy of my record keeping?"

Maureen glared at him. She wouldn't put it past the old relic to fudge things so nothing changed. He, like the others, enjoyed living where the light didn't come. Why, she could never guess.

"Fine. Then you'll oversee the retouching of all two hundred and whatever pieces, since we can't replace them," she commanded and stormed off before she could have the pleasure of his scandalized expression.

They hated her. They'd never say it, of course, because even if they suspected Master Edouard wasn't particularly fond of his new wife either, she was, still, his wife. Their opinion of her was reflected in the cruel glint of their eyes, and the soft pauses and sighs before answering questions she supposed they thought she should know the answer to. *Dear, when you're older, you'll understand.*

And so what if she was only eighteen? Many of her old friends were marrying now, or soon, and starting their own lives. Sure, with men their own ages, but what was age except a limitation or a freedom? Maureen's age had never served her, and so she had no time for it, or for those who would use it against her.

So many nights, Maureen started to lodge her complaints with her husband over dinner. Dinner was the only time they ever spent alone, though it was rarely spent in any companionable way. He read the evening paper, while she picked at her food, waiting for him to set his reading down, even temporarily, so she could broach whatever subject was on her mind.

But Edouard was not a man who would stomach petty disagreements. He had no patience for it when she'd been his employee and she remarked on the cruelty of the other women in the office, and he wouldn't now.

"This one's a little different, Liv. Lizzy just finished it, and she says it's totally out there. Bananas." Maureen made special care of showing Olivia the front and back covers of the book Elizabeth had dropped off earlier that day. Olivia reached for it, but her baby hands were too small to do anything more than brush against the waxed cover. *Carrie* by a man named Stephen King. Maureen had never heard of him. Maureen, who had only ever enjoyed one book when she was living at home, couldn't put them down now. She didn't know about this one. She'd had more than her own share of teenage angst, and was in no hurry to relive any of it, thank you very much. But Lizzy had said, *this one's about a witch, Maureen. Like us. King doesn't exactly call her one, but it's not like average guys know shit about witches. He gets it right, though. You know, the telekinesis or whatever. Wait until you get to the prom scene. You'll wish you could go back to high school just to settle some business.*

Maureen thought this might be too heavy for sweet Olivia, but then, what good had her own sheltered upbringing brought her? The world was hard, and pretending otherwise didn't help your children, it made them unprepared for it.

Still. She thought maybe she finally understood Irish Colleen, a little. Maureen wondered how long until she'd be locking her daughter away from the dangers of the world, too.

There was one thing she wouldn't be able to shelter her from, though, unless she could fix it before Olivia was old enough to be hip to the truth: Maureen's relationship with Olivia's father.

She had time, but Maureen knew well enough how time liked to creep up and catch you by surprise. What felt like years to fix her strange marriage would soon feel like days. It wouldn't be easy to make someone love her, especially when one of the house rules was that she respect that she not seek affection from him.

Maureen really didn't want to anger Edouard. Loveless as their marriage might be, there was a comfortable routine now in the Blanchard household. Even he seemed to have warmed up to their daily thirty minutes in the dining room. He was less stiff, and sometimes even made conversation, however brief. Recently, he'd started to ask about her day, and what Olivia had been up to. She didn't want to disrupt this, or revert things back to the way they were when she'd arrived. Between the joy she got from mothering Olivia and the placid acceptance from her husband, Maureen was starting to feel as if she could find her place in this life her brothers had chosen for her.

Olivia deserved better than comfortable safety, though, and Maureen would find a way to give that to her, even if it did re-freeze the wall of ice between husband and wife.

"FOR THE LOVE OF ALL WE HOLD DEAR, BRAKE SOONER!"

Elizabeth gripped the wheel tighter, glaring at her brother from her peripheral. Last time Augustus barked at her, for running a stop sign—to be fair, she hadn't *seen* it, or of course she would have stopped—she'd fully rotated in her seat to give him a piece of her mind for making her more nervous than she already was. His eyes were round saucers of fear and he demanded she pull over, where he gave her a rousing lecture on never taking her eyes off the road.

"Last time you said I braked too hard! Which is it?"

"It's both, Elizabeth, and if you can't take criticism, then maybe you're not ready for this."

"I don't think you're ready for this. Over there, clutching your chest, like an old woman about to ask for her damn smelling salts."

"I'm not ready to die, if that's what you mean."

Elizabeth made a dramatic show of sitting up bone-straight as she turned on her blinker and very purposely navigated the car onto Seventh with all the flair of a grandmother.

"Better?"

"That attitude doesn't belong behind the wheel of a car." Augustus adjusted his seat belt and grunted. "But yes, better."

"I appreciate you helping me," Elizabeth ventured. She started with a thanks, hoping it would soften the path for what she wanted to say next.

"Fair is fair," Augustus replied. "And you need to learn sometime. If Dad were here, he'd be doing this, but he's not, so that's what you have brothers for."

"You know I'm happy to keep looking after Ekatherina."

"Brake. Brake!" Augustus said. "Lizzy, you need to learn to

watch for stop signs! Saying you didn't see them is not only not an excuse, it's how people get killed."

"I'm hardly even going twenty-five," she muttered. "Anyway, Ekatherina. I know you don't like talking about it."

"I don't like talking about anything when you're supposed to be focused on learning to drive."

Elizabeth wished she could've talked to Connor about this before jumping in with both feet. He always had good advice. But his stupid aunt was a draconian overlord, and worse, she didn't even want the kids there anymore. Now, Thomas was off to another aunt's house in Jackson, Mississippi, and Connor was being shipped to Boston for the rest of the summer, to stay with his cousin Rory, and if their mother wasn't better by fall, the move might become more permanent.

She couldn't even conceive of this being reality. There was no healthy future for Elizabeth that didn't include Connor Sullivan at her side. Long ago, she'd stopped caring about the prophecy she'd seen for him, because to die his wife would be less lonely than to live whatever was left of the rest of her life without the only person in the world who understood her.

Connor would say push forward. He might be fearful of the unknown, but he'd taught her that secrets were poison.

"I can't get you to talk at home," Elizabeth said as she eased into a stop at the big red sign, proud. "So I guess that means we talk here."

"Or you focus on your driving instruction so we both survive this."

"Aggie." Elizabeth hated, *hated* talking about her visions. But sometimes, even if she couldn't change the outcome, she could reduce the collateral damage. In this case, her brother's sanity and happiness. "I'm about to break my own rule. For you."

"I wish you wouldn't," he replied. His body language had shifted. He was tense, and this time, not from her driving.

"Too bad. I'm at the wheel, and unless you want to jump out of a moving vehicle like a maniac, you're stuck listening to what I have to say."

"Elizabeth, I don't want to talk about my wife. I know there are problems. I know she's not well. Talking about it changes none of that."

"She's definitely not well," Elizabeth agreed. "But your daughter is. She should be your focus right now."

"They're both my focus." His right hand reached out and gripped the door handle. "Turn here."

"I'm not ready to go back."

"I am. Turn."

Elizabeth kept going, through the stop sign, toward Magazine. "You *should* focus on your wife, but mainly because of your daughter. You can't have Ekatherina throwing herself down a flight of stairs or anything."

"Elizabeth, *goddammit.*"

"She is not the only thing in your life, Aggie, and she's not even the best thing in your life. You remember that company you built? That magazine everyone loves?"

"I'm serious, Elizabeth."

"You and Connor have something in common. You both think using my name will get me to be more serious. But what I have to say *is* serious, and I'm concerned."

"This isn't concern, this is a coup."

"It's only me here."

"You think I won't jump out?"

"No, I know you won't. Augustus, your company is thriving. I'll admit, I wasn't sure if you were crazy when you said you wanted to launch a damn magazine, but it's taken off, because of *you*. You should be happy about this!"

"I am."

"Bullshit."

"Not everyone has your emotional range."

"Thank God for that."

"I don't need the whole world to know when I've had a good day."

"Well, you can bullshit everyone else, but not me. I know how things end, but for you, there's options for how you come out of it."

"What does that mean?"

"I can't say."

Augustus threw his hands up. "Great. You force me to talk, and now you won't say anything useful." He pointed ahead. "Take this left. We're going back to Magnolia Grace. *Now.*"

Elizabeth obeyed this time. She'd said most of what she needed to say, and what she had left would throw him into giving her the silent treatment anyway.

"You know what she said to me, Aggie? When I told her I was missing Connor?"

"No, and this isn't an invitation to tell me."

"She said, 'When your love is gone, you have permission to love another.' She said that, Aggie. And, you know, I never saw your future when you were in Maine. I don't know why. But two of our siblings, separately, came to me asking about her, and what she was up to when she made you go home without her. I can read between the lines."

"Elizabeth. Stop. Please."

"The kid is yours. She's yours, but that doesn't make what happened in Maine okay. It won't make a bit of difference by the end of this year, either. Take *care* of yourself, Augustus. Your little girl is going to need you, and your business is still going to be there when all the rest is just a memory."

Augustus leapt out of the car before she could ease it all the way into the drive.

Maureen's heart was a racing mess. She was growing colder by the minute and wished she'd had the presence of mind to turn on the heater before leaving all her clothes on the other side of the room. No one in New Orleans ran their heat in the summer, but most of the city embraced the sunlight. Most didn't live, curtains drawn, in the cool darkness.

The rose petals were soft, but they made her itch all over. It had taken her well over an hour to pluck them all from the bouquet she picked up at the florist four blocks down St. Charles, and her fingers were a bloody mess from trying to do it in a hurry. She'd started late, and Edouard would be home any minute now.

Every sound in the house made her curl up in anxiousness. She readjusted her dark hair a dozen times, first draping it over her breasts, then pulling it back, to expose them. She finally settled on covering her breasts, because she had to remember who she was dealing with. Baby steps were required.

Except there was nothing *baby steps* about this, was there? She was nude, atop hundreds of rose petals that would wilt very soon, on *his* bed, where she'd never once been invited before. She was breaking his most important rule, and it was a stretch to hope his arousal at the sight of her would outweigh his wishes.

The front door opened and closed. He always came to his room first, to change out of his office attire and into a less formal, but still stylish outfit of slacks and a collared shirt. Maureen rushed to double-check her body placement, the petals, her hair. In her frenzy, she'd broken into a light sweat, and her hands swiftly wiped at her forehead and the back of her neck. "Oh God, come on, Maureen, pull it together, breathe, breathe!"

His footsteps on the stairs boomed in her ears, blending with the pulse of her growing heartbeat. He always sounded so heavy, as if weighed down, as he ascended, but he never *looked* tired after a day at the office. Edouard was an enigma, and under any other circumstance, one she'd have exactly zero desire to solve. But her daughter deserved a nuclear family, and Maureen wouldn't stop until she'd given her exactly that.

Edouard paused outside the door. Why did he linger? Maureen chanced a glance over her shoulder and noticed she hadn't closed the door all the way. He'd be wondering at that, because the household staff had worked in his employ long enough to know better.

The door creaked open. She waited, listening for a reaction. The silence was a knife in her belly.

"Maureen," he said without stepping in. "What are you doing?"

"I wanted to surprise you," she purred, though her voice was shaking.

"You've done so. You can leave."

Maureen's brow was a sweaty mess. She didn't touch it this time, because she was afraid of matting her hair and destroying the illusion—or what remained of it. She turned, exposing all of herself. He may have discarded her over a year ago, but Maureen knew who she was. She knew precisely how men reacted to her, and even after giving birth to a child, her body was as small and taut as it had ever been.

"Come play with me, Edouard."

"Maureen." Edouard's jaw was tight. He ground his teeth. "What have I said? If you want a child, I require notice."

"I don't want another child. I want you." She rolled her hair back behind her, removing the last layer of cover. She was now entirely raw and vulnerable.

Maureen searched for the telltale bulge in his pants, but found nothing.

Had he a mistress, then? Was that what he'd been doing as the day turned to evening?

Knock it off. Be angry later. Right now, you're on a mission.

Edouard's daze ended. He marched into his closet, and when he came out, he threw a robe at her. It landed in a heavy heap at her side. "Put this on."

"Husband... let me help you unwind."

"Maureen, I'm not playing games with you. Get dressed."

"But I went to all this trouble to please you."

"All you've done is create a mess for the staff to come clean up and make a fool of yourself. What on earth were you thinking with all those dying rose petals?" He shook his head. "Get dressed. Get out. Tell Regina to come in after I've changed."

Maureen's eyes welled with tears. She'd done this to herself, and now both her heart and body were exposed before a man who had never cared for her beyond the fulfillment of his perverted need. And she wasn't even *attracted* to her husband! She was doing this for the greater good, for the sake of her family! He should *be* so lucky as to have a young, virile, supple young woman throwing herself at his feet, with all this extra effort. He had no idea how fortunate he was.

"Please. Don't make me ask again."

Maureen ripped the robe from the bed and rolled off. Rose petals stuck to the back and side of her, but she couldn't stand to be in the same room as Edouard another minute. She shimmied into the satin fabric and cinched the belt so tight her breath caught.

"I'm trying to make this a marriage," she said, her voice warbled with the rise of emotion.

"That's your first mistake," Edouard replied. He peeled a petal from her collarbone, curled his lips in disgust, and tossed it on the ground. "Don't cry on my account. What you're feeling right now was completely unnecessary. All you had to do was remember the rules."

"I just want Olivia to have a normal life."

"Olivia will never want for anything."

"Except a mother and father who love one another."

"Well," Edouard said as he nudged her into the hallway and moved to close the door. "I was raised in a house without that and turned out just fine."

The door clicked shut.

CHAPTER 10

The Arrangement

Colleen summoned everything she knew to be true about herself, her strength, her willpower, her core of being, to pull herself from her bed.

None of those things were more powerful than her all-consuming grief, and she didn't understand *why*. At no point in her life had she ever been a victim of something she couldn't overcome. Not even the losses of her father or Maddy had rendered her so paralyzed.

If this was love, why did she feel like this?

If this was love, how could Noah have walked away so easily?

If this was love, why would anyone in their right mind ever want it?

She missed the deadline for fall registration. One professor called to ask after her, which she knew was not the typical treatment for students. He beseeched her to contact the admissions department as soon as possible, or risk missing a term. He'd sounded really, genuinely concerned, and that only made her feel worse. Even the looming repercussions from this weren't enough to fight the magnet of depression weighting her to her bed.

Noah hadn't called. He hadn't written. Two days after he'd emptied his things from the apartment, she found his favorite shirt, but he'd said nothing about it, or made no attempt to retrieve it, and so now it was her favorite shirt. Or would be, if she could make herself get dressed.

Although Noah wasn't calling, Colleen's phone rang incessantly. Evangeline, mainly, but also her mother, Elizabeth, Maureen, and even her brothers. She knew who was calling because Charles had shipped her this ridiculous contraption called an answering machine, something she'd seen only once or twice, and never in her own home, because such an indulgence would have been insulting to a woman as practical as Irish Colleen. His note had said, *Now you have no excuses when Mom calls, and I don't have to hear about how terrible you are about keeping in touch.*

Irish Colleen's calls were always a surprise, because the long-suffering Deschanel mother viewed long-distance charges as an unnecessary frivolity. Unless someone was dying, a letter would suffice.

The answering machine had long since run out of space on the tape, and Colleen had no inclination to do a thing about it. Now, when the phone rang, she didn't know who was on the other end, and it was better that way. They all knew by now why she hadn't come home. When the phone calls grew more and more worried, Colleen gave Evangeline permission to tell them, so they'd stop worrying and leave her alone. She hadn't wanted them to know about Noah when they were together, and now that they were apart, their knowledge of him stung in a way that made the breakup that much harder. She saw herself through the eyes of her pitying siblings, and there was nothing worse. *Poor Colleen. She tried to love, but it just wasn't meant to be.*

She ignored them.

Their calls.

Their letters, which reminded her that enough time had passed for them to know about her heartbreak and for a letter to arrive from the United States.

Their tender sympathy.

Even Ophelia's letter, which would undoubtedly contain

wisdom she needed, sat unopened in the pile under the mail slot. Her familiar, flourished scrawl burned at Colleen's heart, but it wasn't enough.

Nothing was enough.

The phone rang again.

Colleen wished she had the energy to get up to unplug it.

Instead, she pulled the blankets over her head.

"YES, I'M *FUCKING SERIOUS.* DO YOU NOT REMEMBER OUR talk in the hospital when Nicolas was born?"

Colin grimaced. "I remember you were in a state."

"A state. What the fuck is that? We *live* in a state, Colin, that doesn't make us a goddamn state."

His friend folded his hands over the dark mahogany desk. All around him were richly-colored, leather-bound books Charles doubted Colin would read, but certainly helped set the impression that, like all Sullivan attorneys, he was *esteemed.*

"I don't know why you're yelling at me, Charles."

"I'm not yelling!"

"What does Cordelia say?"

"Who gives a fuck about what Cordelia does or doesn't say?" Charles snorted. He uncrossed his legs and set his other foot atop his knee, leaning back. "If she didn't realize what a stupid decision it was then, she does now."

"How so?"

"I threatened the bitch with divorce."

Colin's eyes widened. "Oh. How did she take it?"

"I don't think the hellbeast grasped that, with my son born legitimately, I don't even fucking need her anymore."

"Yes, but why wouldn't *she* want a divorce, too? Her father is gone, and as you vaguely explained to me before, you only married her to appease some agreement between your dads. Neither of them are here to say anything about it."

Charles threw his hands up. "She's a banshee! Who knows why

Cordelia thinks the way she thinks? I gave up trying to figure out her bad witch routine a long time ago." He rotated legs again, easing a bit. "She, I don't know, gives a shit what society thinks, which makes no sense at all seeing as she treats everyone she comes in contact with like she's a minion of Satan sent to steal their joy."

Colin blinked hard.

"It probably doesn't hurt that she's penniless, too."

"What about her father's company?"

"She sold her shares. Remember?"

"Yes, that's right. We helped her with the transaction."

Charles shrugged. "Wasn't as if there was anything left even if she hadn't sold."

Colin nodded slowly. "So she's motivated to stay, and yet she can't give you more children."

"Can't?" Charles rolled forward in his seat, slapping his hands against the desk, delighting in Colin's light jump. "Let's not pretend the bitch didn't orchestrate an 'emergency' hysterectomy to avoid ever fucking me again."

"Huck, it isn't as if you want to sleep with her, either." Colin's eyes traveled north, as he considered his next words. His face portrayed his search for patience. "Do you really want more children? Is that really what's at play here? Or is this something else?"

Charles wanted to swipe his hand across the desk and send the contents sailing. That might make his point. He didn't have a channel for his frustration, and so it bubbled through the pores of his skin, burning, demanding a better release. "I want a daughter. Don't you dare bring up what I think you're about to bring up, either."

"I wouldn't. Not unless you did first."

"I don't ever want to talk about it. She's not mine. I want one who is." Charles rubbed his index finger over his nose. "I thought Nicolas would help me forget about what happened. About what's *out there.*" He wagged his finger at the window. "He didn't. He's my son, but I didn't lose a son, now, did I?"

Colin's silence was soothing. Charles had always liked his friend best when he listened, resisting the urge to proffer his opinion, which was always superior.

"Even if that bitch Cordelia could have more children, I don't want her infecting the household with more of her tainted genetics. It's going to be enough work for me to exorcise her out of my boy." Charles jumped up and started pacing. "Cordelia can't have children, but we both know who can."

"And Cordelia?"

"Have you been paying attention at all? Who gives a fuck about Cordelia and her feelings? She didn't give a fuck about mine when she had her insides ripped out!"

"You're not worried that having children by your mistress nanny will be a bad look?"

"Not the least bit, because you're going to draw up papers, which I'll take to the bitch to sign, that say if she wants to stay married then she better learn how to be an Oscar-winning actress and claim any children Lisette might have as her own. And if she ever so much as breathes one word to even a single person, she's on the street, and I don't care what happens to her."

"She's still the mother of your child, you know."

"Please don't remind me."

"What about Lisette? Does she have a say in all this?"

Charles grinned. "Lisette and I have already started the needed exercises to get this ball moving."

"She doesn't mind that the world will think her children belong to another woman?"

Charles shrugged. "Pretend you're Lisette Duchene for a moment, Colin. I know you've got a twig and berries under your skirt somewhere, but just go with me. Lisette came from nothing. Sure, we pay her a handsome salary, but imagine if she was the mistress of that same house paying her... if she had more rights than the actual mistress, more freedom, more money, more love. Now imagine she could do it without tying herself down to marriage. Isn't that what women want nowadays anyway? All that feminist women's lib bullshit, about being independent women who don't need no man, or whatever?"

Colin shook his head. "I don't understand why you just don't divorce Cordelia, though. Be with Lisette if that's what you want, and do it as a free man. You hold all the cards here. Cordelia's the one who needs you."

Charles paused behind his chair. He dropped his hands onto the cool leather and leaned in. "I've invested a year into this bitch. A *year*, Colin. I gave up my happiness for her. The least she can do is be a public face for my happy family. And she can do it from the comfort of her own place in New Orleans, and leave me and mine alone." He paused. "My mother dealt with a lot of horrible gossip, a poor woman marrying a rich man. She struggled all our lives with it. Lisette and I can have our family without subjecting her to society's bullshit."

"And Nicolas?"

Charles scoffed. "Nicolas is *my* son. Mine. If Cordelia wanted a kid, she wouldn't have done what she did. Giving birth to him was living up to her end of a bargain we made. That's all he is to her. And you know what? I say, *good.* Lisette is already a better mother in the weeks Nicolas has been in our lives than Cordelia will manage to be in whatever remains of her miserable life. My son won't grow up fatherless, like I did."

"But motherless is okay?"

Charles tapped the leather with his fist. "He won't be motherless. He'll have Lisette."

Colin sighed, a sound Charles would always equate with his own failure in some way. He had the powerful urge to tell him what Catherine tasted like after she'd come. "Are you sure you want to do this?"

"If you're not up to this, I'll ask your dad. Or one of the other cookie-cutter suit-and-tie Sullivans running around the office."

"Cordelia will agree?"

"Her back is in a corner, Colin. She played the one single hand she had, and now there's no going back. She's not as smart as she thinks she is."

Colin scribbled something in his leather notebook. "I just hope you don't live to regret this, Charles."

"Regret is my only constant. She's a fickle cunt, but she's always there for me."

"I can have everything drawn up by the weekend." Colin set his fountain pen neatly to the side. "I'll have paperwork for Lisette, too."

"Lisette? Why?"

"Huck, I know when you're enamored with someone you don't always see clearly."

"The fuck I don't."

"But no one in the firm is going to do this without Lisette also being legally bound to keep this secret. No one knows a thing about her." Colin leaned in. "I mean it. I had her investigated when you hired her."

"You *what*?"

"Standard procedure," Colin explained. "Any time the Deschanels hire someone, the check is compulsory. I did it long before I knew you wanted her to handle the, er, more serious job of bearing your children."

"I see."

"I should hope so, because you're leading this family, and it will be up to you to teach your son to do the same."

"What's that supposed to mean?"

"Anyway," Colin said. "You may love this girl, but you're not some average guy from around the way. You're Charles August Deschanel, fifth descended from the Charles who established the New Orleans Deschanel family and set you on the path for wealth that's hard to accurately calculate, it grows so fast. Anyone who bears your children has to know they are not bearing the children of the same said average guy. Lisette *will* sign documentation promising to maintain the secret as long as you choose to keep it as such, and she *will* sign a document promising never to take any children of yours without your consent, or to ever attempt a grab at custody. We'll take special care to detail any other instances that might need spelled out in the documentation, but this isn't optional. You might think I'm rigid and difficult, but I'm protecting you."

There was no end to Colin's ego, but he hadn't come here for advice. Augustus had provided this already, and once again, had surprised Charles with how much insight his straight-laced brother actually possessed.

You have your heir. No one can question that. What you do from here on out is a matter of your own happiness now. You did your job. Now do what you want.

"Fine."

"Fine? Not going to argue with me?"

Charles exhaled as he shrugged. "What's the point? Legalese is your specialty. Women are mine. You stick to what you do best, and I'll stick to what I do best."

Colin chuckled, looking at him as if he wasn't quite sure whether to take him seriously. "Okay. Give me a few days. Once everything is signed, you're free to do as you please."

Charles smiled. "I'm several steps ahead of you, my friend."

FALL 1975

VACHERIE, LOUISIANA
NEW ORLEANS, LOUISIANA
EDINBURGH, SCOTLAND

CHAPTER 11

Highs and Lows

Nothing prepared Charles for the rush that came from fatherhood.

It was a flood of excitement at every giggle or kick of Nicolas' tiny feet. Dizziness when he trained his expressive eyes on his father. A soft, lilting high when Nicolas fell asleep in his arms, his little mouth parted in a light O.

Nicolas was a delight of innocence and perfection. He was everything Charles wished to be, somewhere within his dark heart, and now he *could* be that, with his son.

Nicolas' fine, wispy hair had begun to darken, not at all like Charles' own dirty blond. Charles frowned at that, until he remembered his father, August, had that dark chestnut hair that lived only in his dreams now. If Nicolas resembled Charles' hero, that was fine by him. And, although the doctor said he was probably imagining it, seeing as it was too early to know for sure, he thought Nicolas' eyes were darkening by the day, too.

He was hardly fussy. Lisette minded him all day and night with soft patience, but even she commented that she expected him to be more trouble. Boys always were, she said, and Charles could believe it. He slept for four or five hours at a time, which meant that

Charles had Lisette to himself for hours before Nicolas required a feeding.

The transition from father to lover was effortless, because the three of them were one happy little family, isolated from the pain and suffering of the world, ensconced in a universe of their own making.

Charles was convinced only men who had never had a son needed drugs. He was going straight. Cocaine would heighten something he wanted to experience exactly on the level it was meant for, and to miss even a single second of fatherhood would be unforgivable.

He didn't think of Catherine anymore.

But there was still the matter of Cordelia to attend to.

Doctoral students had their own assigned seats in the library at the university. Unlike the long tables where undergrad and grad students studied, the assigned desks were covered in varying degrees of personal effects, from pictures to books left overnight. There were only twenty or so at any given time, and the PhD students all worked at their own pace, at their own hours.

Noah had always been a night owl. His mind was sharpest around the witching hour, an irony never lost on Colleen. Many evenings, after they'd exhausted one another with their love, he'd wake and trudge into the dining room in his shorts and tee, glasses on, and make a cuppa while he worked well into the morning. She sometimes found him asleep the next morning, nose pressed into the spine of his textbook.

Colleen still wasn't sleeping. She might never again, if she didn't resume some control over her tattered life. She was grateful the admissions department let her join the fall program late, but now she had the challenge of keeping her grades above water, and for the first time in her life, she wasn't certain she could.

And all the while, her mind churned and over-processed all the memories, tiny and large, inconsequential and powerful. How could that accident have been the end? How did saving his life not outweigh his own prejudices?

Nothing in her mind found the answer to this, and she had to know. She had to know to move on, and there was only one person who could give her what she sought.

Colleen pulled the collar of her trench coat high around her face to block the wind whipping off Arthur's Seat. A low fog hung over the stone streets, hovering right around her ankles. There were few out at this hour, only the pub drunkards stumbling in and out of one establishment after another, and a handful of students, caffeinated and praying for focus.

Her low heels clicked on the stones. The sound echoed in the cool night. She drew closer to the library, where he either would or wouldn't be. Where he either would or wouldn't talk to her.

A whoosh of air yawned as she tugged at the heavy double doors of the library. The sound caused a couple nearby students—undergrads—to turn in curiosity, before surrendering back to their studies. A young woman sat behind the front desk with her feet kicked up, reading a tattered paperback Colleen couldn't see the cover of. Unlike the students, she didn't acknowledge Colleen's intrusion on the quiet night.

Colleen wove her way through the aisles, flanked by stories-tall shelves. The doctoral desks were in the back, near a section of titles that could not be checked out but were available for use to the PhD students at their assigned desks.

The muted, softly echoing sound of feet shuffling as she approached the area gave her pause. Someone was here. Maybe Noah.

Why am I doing this? To carve an even deeper gash in my failing heart?

No, she thought. For the gift of logic that comes with clarity. To know is power, even if the knowing drives an even sharper pain.

Colleen's fingers played with the dried, now crumbling heather band in her pocket. She hadn't been able to make herself part with it, but she knew better than to wear it anymore.

She stepped into a small clearing, where the doctoral desks were. There *was* someone here, but it wasn't Noah. It was a woman Colleen didn't recognize. She was so engrossed in her work she didn't notice Colleen until Colleen drew closer.

"Oh. Hi. Sorry." The young woman pressed a folded paper into the spine of her heavy book and closed it. "Can I help you? You look lost." Her accent was a soft brogue, similar, but not the same, as the Edinburgh locals.

Colleen read between the lines. *You're not one of us.* "I was looking for someone, but doesn't seem like he's here."

The young woman smiled. "Noah, you mean."

Colleen's stomach lurched at the familiar way her love's name came off her tongue. "Yes, but he's not here, so I'll come back when he is."

"I'm Enid," she offered, but didn't stand. "Noah and I are the night owls of the bunch. He's usually here by now, so I don't know where he is."

"I'll just leave him a note."

"I can tell him you came by, too. What was your name?"

"Madeline," Colleen stammered, not knowing why she lied.

"Madeline." Enid smiled. "Pretty. Okay, Madeline. You leave your note, and I'll tell him you came by." She was back to work, the brief interruption forgotten.

Colleen knew which one was his desk, because she'd helped him pick it out when he was accepted into the program. Back then, she'd imagined, on sleepless nights, bringing him some tea to surprise him, or even to give him a brief, but welcome interlude to get him through the night.

She searched around for paper, when she came across an envelope addressed to Noah. The seal had been broken, and the letter shoved messily back inside. Her hand brushed it aside when she caught the return address: New Orleans.

Colleen glanced back at Enid. The young woman was completely immersed in whatever she was studying. She knew better than to read this, but her curiosity, paired with weeks without answers, defied her better sense.

It was a letter from Noah's father.

She glanced around once more before reading.

Noah,

For some time, I've been considering the right words for this letter. They might have been better over the phone, but I think I know my son, and you'd rather have time to digest them. You take after me.

First, you tell me you've met the love of your life and you're marrying her during Christmas break. Then you say she's saved your life, but you can't be with her? Your words don't make any sense.

You might think I'm dense and don't "get" what you've told me, but your old dad has been around New Orleans long enough to know a thing or two about the Deschanels. I've heard the rumors about how they amassed their wealth, among other things. I worried about you, a man of science, and what it might mean should you discover Colleen was "special" like the rest of them. But I never thought you'd react this way.

I should have written this sooner. When we spoke on the phone, after your accident, I was too relieved that you'd walked away from the crash to process the rest of your news. I can't delay any longer, though. My fear is that my own prejudices may have affected you too much and cost you happiness.

When I told you about your mother being a witch, there was no exaggeration in my words. Her connection with nature went beyond a love of it and what she and her kin could do... things I can't begin to describe to you. In the beginning, I loved her in spite of it. I couldn't help but love Deirdre. She radiated with a force that brought smiles to everyone around her. Eventually, over time, I grew afraid of her and what I could never understand. At the time, I convinced myself her influence would contaminate you and your sisters. I know better now. My greatest regret in life was leaving your mother and my three daughters behind in Ireland. The barter for my pride became a false economy that no longer exists in my middle age. I loved her for who she was, not what she could do. I still love her and always will.

When Colleen laid her hands on you, she did so out of love. Think about those words, Noah. Decide what they mean to you, if anything.

I love you, son. I have always and always will. I only want what is best for you.

Love,

Dad

Colleen's hands were shaking when she shoved the letter back inside. She finally gave up and dropped it on the desk, rushing through the long aisles of the library toward the door and the outside, and the air she so desperately needed.

She doubled over when the cool fog filled her lungs. She gasped, drawing in more, pushing out whatever else was still trapped within her.

Noah's father had said exactly what Noah needed to hear, and still, Noah hadn't called.

It was over. Nothing she could say was even half as important as the elder Jameson pouring his heart out.

Her hand connected with the heather band. She should go back in and leave it. He'd know it was her who'd come. Madeline was a bad lie, and one he'd see through immediately. Leaving the band would at least give them both closure—or her, anyway, seeing as he'd clearly moved on long ago and was doing just fine. Noah and Enid, thick as thieves in their midnight study sessions.

"This is mine," she whispered. A white cloud blossomed in the night before her. "You took my heart. You can't have this, too."

• • •

Cordelia dropped her bags at the foot of the stairs. She shot an impatient, crude look at Richard, who rushed to collect them.

"No," Charles commanded from the top of the staircase. "She can carry her own shit from now on."

Richard disappeared again.

"You're a fool," Cordelia hissed. "This can't work. You're just too stupid to realize it."

"Stupid? Stupid is cutting out the only power you had over me," Charles said. "Stupid is thinking that *I* would never find out about the backroom deal you made with the doctor to pretend you actually needed the surgery. Stupid is not helping your nitwit brother fix your father's company so you had at least something to fall back on." He descended a step. "You know what I am? I'm a fucking charitable motherfucker, that's what I am. I'm the man who could throw you on the street and instead is giving you an allowance bigger than the GDP of New Orleans, and the ability to save face, which is *so* important to you. I'm giving you everything, when you gave me nothing."

Her gray eyes narrowed. "I gave you a son."

"Yes. He's mine," Charles agreed. "Don't forget it."

Cordelia bent at the knee and lifted her heavy bags. Her arms shook with the weight. "Be very sure this is what you want, Charles. This is nothing short of a declaration of war."

He smiled. "A war you can't win."

"A war your *children* will bear most of the losses from."

"My children will be just fine, here, away from you."

"I'll be back," Cordelia said, flashing a grin wider than his, darker than any expression she'd ever worn. "If you want my agreement, I'll be back in this house as I please, when I please. I'll see my son. And I will see whatever bastards you manage to bear with that child upstairs. And they *will* regret the day they were born into this sick arrangement, because suffer they will, Charles. I will take them to public dinners and pretend they are mine when we entertain, but their private lives will be hell. And I will make damn sure they know exactly who to thank."

Condoleezza opened the door to let Cordelia through, and then closed, and locked it, when she was gone.

"Change the locks," Charles gruffed.

CHAPTER 12

Dreamers

Augustus had never been a man who went somewhere when he slept. Even as a young man growing up in a colorful household, his sleep had mostly been dreamless. Irish Colleen told him he had fever dreams when he was sick, but he never remembered those. He never remembered anything once his head hit the pillow, and when he woke the following day, he was always refreshed. Unencumbered. Ready to attack the day ahead.

In his short, tumultuous marriage to Ekatherina, Augustus had begun to go places when he slept. In what he now referred to as the Maine Era, his sleeplessness started with images of his wife dancing in another man's arms; a man he refused to give name to, lest he wrest any more power from Augustus' fragile relationship. When she returned, they stopped for a while, but when they learned she was pregnant, his dreams not only returned, but with a vengeance.

Ekatherina, hurling herself off the side of a building, into a dense fog.

Ekatherina, jabbing a butcher knife into her protruding belly, smiling.

Ekatherina, mixing rat poison into her morning coffee, stirring with flourish.

Every night, Augustus was greeted with some new and terrible way his wife devised to take the life of their child, and herself with it. Some nights were more creative, like the one where she gorged herself on so much food she actually exploded, blood and gore spraying the room in bits of horror. In another, she quietly climbed into a cage with hungry leopards.

If Madeline were here, she would've known immediately something was off in his constitution. She used to tell him that he rarely ebbed or flowed at all, and that only a few times in their lives had he ever registered on her "empath radar," as she liked to call it. He was so even, she said, that when something upset him it was like being smacked with a brick, she felt it so keenly. He wondered if what he was experiencing now would feel more like a house landing on her.

But they all had some degree of natural empathy, did they not? Evangeline had called four times in the past week, when she couldn't be bothered to call once a month ordinarily. Charles invited him for lunch twice, declaring he rather liked the last one and they should make a routine of it. Elizabeth couldn't stop herself, it seemed, from constantly sharing her feelings more openly, and if he didn't need her too much—if he didn't fear she was *right* about Ekatherina, right about it all—he'd send her home. She practically lived there now, having made a point to catch up with her studies in the summer so she could devote her time to helping her brother.

Only Colleen had refrained from reaching out, and that made him worry about *her.* Evangeline said she was nursing a heartbreak, but she'd switched herself off quite neatly with Rory and that professor. This was different, and, for once, Colleen needed him and he was in no position to offer anything.

If he couldn't fix his wife, how could he fix his sister?

Thinking again of Madeline, his success in saving anyone from themselves was dismal.

Elizabeth was in the kitchen making breakfast. Egg shells, cracked in haphazard messes, lay on the counter, and whatever she was making in the pan no longer resembled food. She dipped a spatula in, frowning, and then raced across the room to retrieve her toast, which was now releasing billows of dark smoke into the air.

"I have a housekeeper for that," Augustus chided, though it lacked any energy.

"Don't let Mama hear you talking about letting a stranger make your food," Elizabeth said as she raced her black toast to the garbage. "She already thinks she failed with Charles."

"She married a Deschanel. She knew what she was getting herself into."

"And fought it every step."

"Here. I'll help." Augustus nudged her out of the way and grabbed the pan, carrying it to the garbage. He ignored her offended, *hey*, and then went to crack two more eggs more neatly into the pan. "How did you want them?"

"Scrambled," she conceded. "But make it four eggs. Half were for your wife."

"She wants them scrambled, too?"

Elizabeth wrinkled her nose. "You don't know how your wife takes her eggs?" After an awkward beat, she said, "Yeah, scrambled for both of us."

"Go make the toast. Mind you don't burn it this time?"

"Ha. Ha." Elizabeth marched to the other side and stood sentry at the toaster oven. "I could've done it myself."

"I've grown fond of Magnolia Grace and don't really want to see it burned to the ground."

"This stubborn old monster? Would take more than a kitchen fire."

"She's eating, then?"

Elizabeth leaned into the counter with a shrug. "Sometimes. Sometimes she ignores it. One time she threw the whole plate across the room. That's why I switched to scrambled. Have you ever tried to get egg yolk out of burgundy wallpaper?"

Augustus divided the eggs onto two plates. An image of old Mr.

Rochester's forgotten, lunatic wife appeared in his head and he dismissed it summarily. "Thanks for being patient, Lizzy. I know it's not easy."

"She's family, whether she likes it or not." Elizabeth turned to pull the toast out, but her hand, and the bread, hovered in midair. She went rigid. "Aggie." Her voice dropped to a whisper. "Aggie, come here. Now. But quietly."

A sheet of ice hardened in his veins. He appeared behind his sister and started to ask, but then he saw.

Ekatherina, her pale blue nightgown billowing out around her, climbing over the banister from the second floor.

"Jesus," he whispered. He set the rag aside and stepped carefully around Elizabeth. "Stay here."

"Maybe she's sleepwalking."

"We're past making things up, Lizzy. You know that."

"Yeah." Elizabeth followed him despite what he'd asked. "I'll grab a pile of towels."

"Towels?"

"In case she jumps."

"Jesus," he said again, as the very dream he was now living came back to him. *Ekatherina, arms wide, flying from the banister.* "She's not jumping. She can't."

"I know," Elizabeth said, but scurried to get the towels anyway.

Augustus tiptoed across the wood floor. Ekatherina wasn't sleepwalking, but she did seem to be in some sort of fugue state, and she hadn't noticed him yet. There was still the entire foyer and two dozen steps separating them. A whole world of events could pass in that space, and he'd be helpless to stop any of them.

His arms hovered out at his sides, and he didn't know why. They wouldn't make noise, but he feared even touching himself would draw attention. Ekatherina had one leg over, but was struggling to get the second one over. She was tiny, and the banister tall, and it would take some doing.

Augustus made it to the base of the staircase before Elizabeth appeared with a deep pile of towels that towered over her. He loved his sister in that moment. It would take a thousand towels to save Ekatherina from what she intended to do to herself, but Elizabeth wouldn't stand by idly. She'd endured her sister-in-law's torrent of moods for months, and if anyone knew how serious this threat was, it was her.

But then he discovered there was a different sort of brilliance to Elizabeth's plan.

Ekatherina noticed her and paused with a scowl. "What you do with towels?"

"We're out upstairs."

"No, we are not."

"How would you know? You never get out of bed."

Ekatherina pouted. "You never like me. Just a spy for husband."

From the corner of his eye, he saw one tiny hand emerge from the towels and, almost imperceptibly, urge him to go.

Augustus didn't dare look at Elizabeth, but he understood. The distraction wouldn't last long. He couldn't waste it.

"In America, we call it being sisterly."

"America. In America. What so good about America?"

"You tell me, lady. You're the one who moved here for a better life."

Augustus paused several steps up, tensing. Elizabeth needed to be careful with her words, but he couldn't risk saying anything, so he continued.

How did it come to this? His familiar, daily refrain. The only words he knew to ask anymore, because to dig any deeper would bring forth answers he wasn't ready for.

"Do you see better life?" Ekatherina waved one hand around. The other clutched the banister. Augustus took this as a good sign. If she wanted to fall, she'd let go. She wouldn't be holding so tightly.

"I see you married a man who would do anything for you," Elizabeth said.

Ekatherina laughed. "You don't know. You no marry him."

Elizabeth dropped the towels. She shook her sore arms out. "Look, no, I did not marry my brother, nor do I intend to, but he's been nothing but good to you." Just then, a brief flick of her eyes gave her away, and Ekatherina screamed.

Augustus ran the last few steps and wrapped his arms around her just as she was bending over the railing.

"Ekatherina, I don't understand. Why? Why?"

She kicked and screamed in his arms, but he held fast. Elizabeth raced up the stairs and joined them, wrapping her own arms around the hysterical waif.

"You never understand anything! You never did!"

Elizabeth passed a look over the thrashing woman. It said, *you'll find no logic in this house, and will only be worse off for seeking it.* "I'll get the syrup."

"You drug me!" Ekatherina's arm broke free and she hit Augustus so hard in the face he saw stars. "You hate me!"

"I love you," he said weakly, holding tight despite the pain radiating behind his eyes, "but I won't allow you to hurt yourself anymore, and I'll be damned if I allow you to harm our daughter!"

With a newfound burst of strength, Augustus lifted her into his arms and carried her into the bedroom.

CHARLES WAS LYING ON THE NURSERY FLOOR WITH Nicolas when Richard interrupted him to say he had a call.

"I'm busy," he replied, in the same singsong voice he reserved for his son. He tickled Nicolas on the tummy, and Nicolas *almost* laughed. He wanted to, Charles could feel it as he watched his son's tiny mouth open wide in delight. "You know I don't want calls when he's awake."

"I do know, but..." Richard twisted his mouth and sighed. "This might be the exception you'd make."

"There are no exceptions, unless someone is dying," Charles said, without taking his eyes off his son, who was now marveling at something on the wall.

"Not even for Catherine?"

All the blood inside of Charles rushed to his head. A sharp, metallic taste filled his mouth. "My Catherine?" He could say this to Richard. Richard knew.

"Your Catherine," Richard said and left, because they both knew there was no further argument to be had.

CATHERINE BEGGED HIM TO MEET HER. SHE NEEDED TO talk to him, but in person, not on the phone. She said this as if she believed her phone calls were being monitored, and he wondered where this paranoia had come from.

"I'm with my son," he said and hated how weak that felt compared to her need of him. Nothing should be stronger than his love for Nicolas, and only Catherine could show up to test that.

"Please, Huck." She sobbed on the other end. "I won't take much time from you. I promise."

"Okay, uh..." Charles blew out a breath and looked around. "You can't come to Ophélie."

"Why not?"

"Cordelia," he lied. "Meet me at my flat on Frenchmen. You remember how to get there?"

Tiny exhale from her side. A sob followed. "I could never forget."

CATHERINE WAS A HYSTERICAL MESS. SHE WAS LEAVING Colin, she said, and going to her mother's, though it took ten minutes to pull these basic pieces of information from her, as she paced around the apartment, reaching for pillows, coasters, anything to wrap her hands around and throw.

This hadn't been their place, not like Ophélie, but Charles had taken her here enough times for her ghost to haunt the flat nonetheless. Years, now, since he had seen her step across his oriental carpets; since she'd looked up at him from his bed down the hall.

Mascara ran haphazard lines down her cheeks. She picked up a vase, and this time he went to her, closing his hands around the delicate china and setting it aside.

"Sit down," Charles encouraged, as much for his own nerves as hers.

Catherine sat and then bounced right back up. He decided to sit anyway, because chasing her around the room was too exhausting, and he was already behind on sleep.

"Do you want a drink, then? Something?"

Catherine dropped her hands to her sides. "A drink?"

"Yeah, you know, booze. The shit that might help you calm down."

"I'm *breastfeeding.*"

"Right." Charles blew out a breath. Strike one.

"And maybe I don't need to calm down! Maybe it's my turn to be upset, to have *feelings* for a change. You ever think of that?"

"You talking to me, or Colin?"

"Fuck you, Charles!"

"Cat. You called me."

"Who else was I going to call?"

"Anyone else. Literally *anyone* else," he said and was surprised at himself, at his boldness. Even now, he was caught in her spell. He hadn't stopped loving her, he'd just had other things on his mind, and he could see now that he loved her as much as he ever had.

But he was different now. Changed. Hardened by the decisions he'd made and been asked to make. Before him stood not the angel of his dreams, but the devil he'd chosen for his side before she'd spurned him. He both loved and hated her as she chose him, once again, to be her temporary need rather than her permanent one.

"Well, for your information, I did call my mother," she said, raising both brows as if expecting an accolade.

"Is that where Oz is?"

"What?"

"Your son?"

"I know who Oz is, Huck." She walked into the kitchen and grabbed a stack of napkins from the cozy. She shoved a handful at her nose. "And yes, he's at Mom's. Colin will probably have something to say about *that*, too."

"No matter what happened between you, Colin is his father. And a good one."

Catherine tossed her wad of snotty napkins in the sink. "And when did *you* become so reasonable? You sound like him, you know."

"If that's your idea of an insult, rewind and try again."

Catherine shot him a hard look, eyes narrowing. "Don't tell me fatherhood changed you."

"Okay." He threw his hands up. "I won't, then."

"It did, didn't it?"

"I haven't touched drugs in weeks."

Catherine laughed. "I have a bridge to sell you."

"I'm serious. It was rough at first, but I didn't like how it made me feel when I was with Nicolas. I wanted to be present, I guess. In the moment. With him." He didn't tell her about the weeks of painful, agonizing withdrawals; how he sought out a younger cousin, Luther, to heal him so he'd be less tempted to go back to the way things were.

She crossed her arms. "But you didn't with me?"

"Sorry?"

"You were always loaded to the hilt when we were fucking, Charles, so, what, you never wanted to be present with me?"

Charles shot to his feet. He marched into the kitchen and grabbed her arms. He stopped short of shaking her, though he wanted to. "Why did you call me, Catherine? *Why me*?"

Catherine's face erupted again into pure agony. She went soft in his grip, and he felt like a big, terrible thug in that moment, terrorizing her in her pain.

"Cat. I'm sorry..."

She buried her face in his chest. Her arms slithered up his sides and looped around his neck. "You're the only one, Huck," she sobbed.

"The only what?"

"The only one who understands me." She wiped her face against the cotton of his shirt. "The only one who wants to."

No. No, no, no, he thought, *this is the same trap, the most familiar trap that only Catherine could lay.* She knew now, as she always had, the way to breach his defenses, which were never all that strong to begin with. But if was different now that she was married. Charles didn't think much of marriage when his name was the one on the certificate, but he respected Colin and he wouldn't do this. He *couldn't* do this, no matter how good it felt to have her hands touching the soft flesh of his neck. Or her lips grazing the inside of his collar, sending chills all through him.

"Damn it all," he whispered just before he pressed his mouth to hers. "Damn it all, all of it," he said louder as he lifted the weeping love of his life into his arms and carried her down the hall.

AUGUSTUS WAS LOST TO HIMSELF. HIS TEARS WEREN'T for his wife, or even himself, but for a helplessness he could never reconcile.

He leaned over the kitchen table, face in his arms, and the tears flowed freely. They weren't welcome, but he didn't possess whatever was required to stop them. Not this time.

Elizabeth appeared in the doorway. She didn't say anything, but he heard her soft steps as she drew nearer to him. She paused behind him. Both hands pressed into his back, and then her own face was nuzzled in between his shoulder blades as she knelt behind him in silence.

Augustus cried as his baby sister held him.

CHAPTER 13

Wish You Were Here

Elizabeth waited until Ekatherina was actually asleep before she hesitantly slipped from the room. The embittered woman—whom Elizabeth no longer recognized, for whatever hatred and resentment brewed within her had bubbled to the surface and marred her soft beauty—started to pretend to sleep so Elizabeth would leave. She wasn't very good at it, but even that she *would* do it was enough to send Elizabeth's anxiety through the roof. Why else would she fake it, except to try that same, terrible thing again?

Ekatherina was a terrible actress, so Elizabeth knew what to look and listen for. She might have been better at snowing Elizabeth's brother, but they were well past that.

Aggie, I know you don't want to, but you have to consider committing her.

Lizzy, no. I won't lock up my wife.

She did what she did when we were both home. We were home. *What else is she capable of when we're in the bathroom? Just down the hall for a minute? She's determined to harm herself, and we're not equipped for this.*

You can go. You didn't sign up for this.

I'm not going, and I did sign up for this. You're my brother.

Augustus reluctantly left for work an hour after they'd gotten Ekatherina sedated, but she didn't need to see his future to know he wasn't getting a thing done. His business would suffer because of her, and Ekatherina didn't care. She was a selfish, petulant child who had thrown Elizabeth's brother's world into complete chaos, and she had to make herself not hate the woman for it. Hate was not an emotion suitable for the environment around a pregnant woman, no matter what she'd done.

Ekatherina's future was no longer available to Elizabeth. She'd seen what she'd seen, months ago, and then nothing. She thought she knew why, but it didn't make the minutes any less nail-biting and fearful. What if she found Ekatherina with a knife? What if she drank cleaning solution? What if, what if, what if?

Elizabeth wasn't going far, in any case. The study Augustus had set up for his wife, the one she'd never used, was just next door to her room. Elizabeth slipped inside and closed the door, but she pulled the phone as close to the wall as possible. The walls in this old house were thick as concrete, but the aging wood floors told many tales, and she should hear if Ekatherina got out of bed.

She fished the crinkled paper from her jeans pocket. Rory and Carolina's phone number, in Boston. Cradling the receiver against her shoulder, Lizzy lifted the heavy rotary phone into her lap and pulled the series of numbers around the ring.

Please, please answer. I know I said I could be brave for us both, but I lied. I lied, I lied, I lied and I need you, Connor. I need you ten times harder than any of the times I said I didn't.

"Sullivan residence."

"Rory?"

"Yes, this is Rory Sullivan."

"Hey, it's Lizzy. Lizzy Deschanel."

"Elizabeth! How are you?" More muffled: "Carolina, dear, it's Lizzy!"

"I've been calling for a week, looking for Connor."

"Oh, I'm sorry about that. My class hours are all over the place, and Carolina is usually too busy with Clancy to answer." Something shifted in the background. It sounded like Rory was sitting. "You said you're looking for Connor?"

Why did he sound surprised? The whole universe knew about the two of them. *Connor and Lizzy, like peanut butter and jelly,* was the saying, and when they finally switched to dating from friendship, no one was the least bit surprised or even excited for them. It was assumed it would happen eventually, when the two of them realized what everyone else had for years. "Yeah. He around?"

"No... he's been out all day, right, Car?"

"Out with friends, I think he said," Elizabeth heard Carolina reply faintly from the background.

"Right. Right." A scratching sound overwhelmed the phone as Rory ran his hands over his stubble. "I can tell him you called."

"Please," Elizabeth said. Her pulse was so erratic she almost dropped the phone. She needed to calm down, for her own sake. "Who is he with, did you say?"

"Oh, uh, I think he said Van. Or Vanessa? Vanessa sounds right."

Carolina called something out that Elizbeth didn't hear this time.

"Well, whatever. Friends are friends," Rory said, to them both. "How are you anyway, Elizabeth? How's the family?"

Colleen, you mean? "They're fine," Elizabeth said and hung up the phone.

She froze at the sound of creaking floorboards. Ekatherina. Her rising anxiety glued her to the leather chair, but her pain at the news of Connor was more powerful and she launched forward.

Vanessa. Who was Vanessa? The girlfriend of one of his friends, maybe? Were there dudes named Vanessa?

Don't be a damn fool. Why would he pine over damaged, drug-addled Lizzy Deschanel when he could have a sweet, wholesome, normal girl? She probably glows like sunlight in the rain.

Stop. You don't know anything about this situation. You're gonna make yourself sick with stress.

Too late.

Elizabeth gripped the doorframe, torn between her fears of what had changed in Boston, and what was brewing in the bedroom next door.

If Connor had moved on—*stop, stop it, stop doing this to yourself*—then who was he grieving in her visions? It couldn't be Vanessa, or anyone else. Elizabeth had always been comforted, in a strange way, at the idea of being Connor's dead wife. It means she would die young, yes, but it also meant she would live before she did.

Unless it wasn't her at all.

"Elizabeth! Eggs!"

Elizabeth choked on her breath as she exhaled. A sob trapped inside her, stifling both her emotions and her sense of self.

"Coming!" she cried, voice cracking.

"And *this* is what Mommy will use to seduce Daddy!"

Maureen jumped off the bed and modeled her black negligee for Olivia, who she imagined was very approving of her fashion choice. In her mind, Olivia was not only on her side, but a silent conspirator. In a way, this was true. Olivia might turn out to be the only thing Maureen and Edouard had in common, in the end, but would it be enough?

"He didn't like the roses."

Olivia's face wrinkled with gas.

"I know, Livvy. I *know.* That's what I said, too. What's his problem, anyway?"

Maureen paused before the mirror of her vanity. No lines. Not that she should have them, but there were days she felt like eighteen going on ninety, and one day she fully expected to walk past her reflection and see evidence of this.

Olivia's soft coos drew her attention back to the bed. Her daughter was reaching for her toes, but not quite catching them. She vowed to write it in her baby book, when she finally won the battle.

"I know, sweet darling, I wanted you to have a play date with Nicolas, too. Where *is* your Uncle Charles, anyway?"

Maureen had found her forgiveness of Charles in their shared experiences as new parents. The two least likely caregivers were the only ones traversing this strange landscape, and she liked listening to him talk about Nicolas' messy burping sessions, or his wild urination painting the nursery. She liked talking about Olivia's own little tics, like the way she could transfix on something and stare at it for hours if Maureen didn't stop her.

He was supposed to be there over an hour ago with Nicolas, but he hadn't shown and hadn't called.

"Where is he?" she repeated.

Maureen secretly hoped he might give her advice where her husband was concerned, too. Never mind that Charles had orchestrated this failed marriage. She was past that. For Olivia, she must be past that, because this was Olivia's family, and Maureen was determined to stitch it together into something resembling normalcy. Maureen was utterly convinced that growing up without a father is what had turned her into a teenage sex queen, and she would do everything in her power to keep Olivia from the same future.

She had fantasies of all the little Deschanel babies growing up best friends. Nicolas and Olivia, and Augustus' daughter, whom he would probably name Maddy and make it weird for everyone. Colleen might eventually have kids, if she could get over herself, and Lizzy and Connor were playing with fire. If Edouard didn't have time for Olivia, she would have other men in her life to pick up the baton to mentor Olivia. Uncle Charles, Uncle Augustus. Probably one day, an uncle named Connor, and if Colleen could stop driving men away, there'd been an uncle there, too.

Not for Evangeline, though. Everyone knew she was gay, even if she hadn't embraced the fact herself. Maureen wondered if that's why she'd fled north, to be with more like her.

A chorus of ringing filled the house. It only made the rounds twice, before someone on the staff answered the phone.

"Hell's bells, that better be your uncle saying he has a flat or something!"

The phone was for her, as it turned out, but it wasn't Charles. Maureen handed the baby to Georgia and lifted the receiver.

"Mistress Blanchard speaking."

Tears on the other end. Incoherent blathering.

"I said, Mistress Blanchard. How can I help you?"

"Maureen… it's Lizzy."

"Lizzy, are you okay?"

"No."

Maureen bit her lip. She and Elizabeth had never been close, but the foreboding sense that her sister needed her was so powerful, like the day she sent for Elizabeth to help *her*. "What's wrong?"

"I don't want to be alone right now." Elizabeth sniffled and she shuffled her head against the phone. "No, that's not right. I can't be alone."

Maureen's spine stiffened with purpose. "Where are you?"

"Magnolia Grace. I can't leave. Ekatherina is…"

"Stay put. Olivia and I will be there in ten, and we'll put on some tea and all will be right."

Maureen pulled Olivia back from the housemaid. "Get me a towncar with a car seat, please."

"Yes, ma'am."

"And if my brother, by the grace of God, ever shows up, tell him where I went."

"Yes, ma'am."

Maureen thought for a moment. She knew more about Elizabeth's problems than Elizabeth realized. She'd seen what was in Lizzy's closet, and she thought she knew why. But who was she to judge after all she'd done? Everyone had their escapes, and they were either more or less effective. Lizzy had found hers in copying her oldest brother.

Would Charles ever forgive himself if he knew this?

"On second thought, tell him nothing. He made me wait, and

he can do the same." She bounced Olivia and added, "And say nothing to Edouard if I'm not home for dinner."

"Nothing, ma'am?"

"Nothing," she repeated. "Let him wonder where I stand for a change."

CHAPTER 14

Over My Head

Charles promised himself this wouldn't happen again. It was a promise he believed in. One he lived by, that got him through the long days as Cordelia's husband. It ushered him safely through parties where he and Cat were both in attendance, and made pleasant conversation, when Colin was present, almost easy. The promise sustained him, because it was one that came also with an excruciatingly hard truth: *this* was impossible. Whatever fantasies he'd harbored, years before, of a life with Catherine Connelly, they were just that. She might slink back from her need of him from time to time, but she would never choose him. In her choice was his strength.

Two weeks later, looking down at her peaceful face as she slept in his bed, blond hairs falling and sticking around her mouth, Charles was no longer strong.

Augustus stared at the phone. All he had to do was reach forward and lift the receiver, then dial. It was as simple as that. Augustus liked simple. He detested easy, but simple was a matter of efficiency. Efficiency led to success. Success led to...

He buried his face in his hands. This wasn't business. This was his life.

His unborn daughter's life.

Elizabeth would be babysitting upstairs for a couple more hours before it was his turn to take over. There wasn't much risk of her coming downstairs. She almost never left Ekatherina alone now, not since that day.

And even if she did overhear him, what of it? Ekatherina's mental state wasn't some closeted family secret. If anyone knew the desperation seeping through his veins right now, it was his youngest sister.

Augustus, finally, understood why men resorted to drink.

He felt so old. So terribly, unutterably *old.* He was only twenty-four, and already he'd launched a successful business, married for love, and was now preparing for what might be the end of his marriage, for whatever the opposite of love was.

For her, anyway. He still loved her, despite everything.

At twenty-four, he'd already done so much, but the only thing that mattered to him now was the one thing he hadn't yet.

His daughter still had several months before she'd enter this world.

And he couldn't live in a world where she didn't.

CHARLES TOLD COLIN HE WOULDN'T DIVORCE Cordelia, but he'd said so knowing what his circumstances were. He could never marry Lisette, and in any case, he didn't want to. Somewhere within him, he knew the love he carried for his French nymphet wasn't the lasting kind. It wasn't the Catherine kind.

For Catherine, he would've divorced Cordelia in a heartbeat.

But that wasn't so simple, either, now was it? To choose Catherine would be to lose Colin forever. Of the two, only Colin had ever really been loyal to Charles. He showed tough love at times, and his truths were not always welcome, but these things came from a friendship that had interlaced their entire lives. Cat was only as loyal as her fears allowed her to be.

Now, she was giving him the choice again, and he was no longer strong enough to be sure he'd make the right one.

Since the night she came to him, desperate and seeking his arms, he'd spent his nights making love to her on Frenchmen, and his days enjoying the soft thrill of fatherhood, with Nicolas. It was the best of both worlds. His two loves. His only true loves.

Late at night, while she slept, he'd step out onto the balcony of his flat, listening to the lively beat of jazz float up from the street below as he smoked, and his fantasies would lie to him. They'd show him a world where he could have her, have Nicolas, have Colin, have it all, all of it. Evenings in New Orleans were a place where magic had no counterweight. Where anything was possible.

And then Colin would call him, devastated. He'd ask for advice on how to bring his wife home, as Charles looked over at that same wife, sleeping in his bed, not Colin's.

Catherine's smooth arms rolled around his waist from behind, looping together at his torso. Her face fell against his back, sighing. "I just want it to stay like this, forever."

Charles blew out his smoke, leaning his head back. "Me too."

"It could, you know."

He flicked his butt and redirected his hands to hers, winding their fingers together. "I guess anything is possible."

"What's wrong, Huck? You're changing."

He watched a couple on the street below stumble drunkenly into an overflowing dumpster. "Not the first time you've said that to me."

"I meant you're changing *now.* Right before my eyes. You're not the same man who carried me to bed when I came to you."

He chuckled. His heart wasn't in it, but it felt like the right thing to do. "It's only that anytime you're mine, there comes a point where reality comes in and reminds me the cost of having you."

Catherine dropped her arms. "The cost? What does that mean?"

"Come on. We're not *kids* anymore, Cat."

"We were never kids together."

"Weren't we?" He turned toward her, leaning into the iron balcony. "And now we both have children, Catherine."

"Catherine!" Her mouth and eyes widened with offense. "Now I'm Catherine?"

Charles lit another cigarette. It wasn't what he *really* wanted, but he'd made a promise to Nicolas, and what greater promise was there, than the one you made to your son? "Don't read so much into everything. I'm not that deep."

"So, what, I'm just a fling to you? Something you turn to when you have a need?"

His laugh this time was real. "Quit it. I have much easier, less heartbreaking ways to fulfill my needs, and we both know it. Don't put words in my mouth, or intentions in my heart."

"Poetic," she accused.

"I have changed," he said. "I've changed because of you. I've changed away from you, and I've changed for reasons that have nothing to do with you. One thing, though, will never change."

She curled her lips in petulant defiance.

"That I love you more than my own life." He tangled his hands in her messy blond hair, careful not to burn her with his cigarette. His face lowered to hers. "That you'd ever question this hurts me more than I can say."

Tears spilled over and rolled down her cheeks. "You're saying goodbye again, aren't you?"

Charles kissed her. His hands fell to her sides, to the thin fabric on her negligee. "Soon," he whispered against her lips. "But not tonight."

THE DIAL TONE GRATED HIS EARS IN THE QUIET ROOM. The sound was repellent, and he wanted it gone, but he had to dial.

Augustus realized he didn't know who he planned to call.

Charles was entangled in some secret tryst with Catherine Sullivan, something he only knew because Lizzy knew, and Lizzy knew because she'd seen something about that and wasn't telling.

Evangeline was out of the question. She was gone for a reason, and he'd pushed her to do it, for her own good. He couldn't reel her back in now.

Maureen was... well, of all of them, she was the least capable of the kind of reasoning he required. She'd been over at the house a lot lately, visiting with Elizabeth, which struck Augustus as extremely odd, but he said nothing. He was afraid of what Ekatherina would do, too, and he understood the need to share that burden.

Mama was out of the question.

This left Colleen, who was herself drowning in her own heartache. Augustus' guilt gnawed around the corners of his own conundrum. He'd called her a few times to check in, of course, but he never really expected her to answer, or to talk about what had happened to her. He'd called her out of love, and duty, but the truth was, he wasn't equipped to help her any more than he was able to help himself. He'd been relieved when she never answered, and then angry at himself for failing her.

Augustus found himself dialing Scotland anyway.

CHARLES AND CATHERINE WOKE AROUND THE SAME TIME. Like all mornings during the period of their time-bending interlude, they each went about dressing on their own, keeping their peace, and parted with simply a kiss. Any more than that felt disrespectful to what was next on their agenda, which in both their cases, was always a day with their children.

Catherine, to her mother's house.

Charles, to his.

It was somewhere around the first week he realized he looked forward more to the days than the nights. By the end of the second, he wasn't thinking of her at all when he was on the floor of his son's nursery, being silly and playful.

He kept that to himself, but wondered if she felt the same way when she was with Oz.

Charles hoped she did, but he feared otherwise.

There was also Lisette to consider. She asked only once where he'd been going, but she knew, in the way all women knew. Would she be as receptive to him when he came home for good? Should she? He didn't deserve it, but her options were limited. What was most likely was that she would love him out of necessity.

Catherine. Cordelia. Lisette. All the women in his life were so very different and served very different purposes in his sphere of living.

None belonged there.

"Should I have the staff save you a plate?" Lisette asked, eyes hopeful, when he left that day, handing Nicolas back to her.

"Not tonight," he said. "But soon."

Colleen answered the phone.

Augustus didn't waste time with pleasantries, or small talk. Neither liked it much, and if he stalled in any way, he might never say what he needed to.

That he was afraid.

That he, the man who had never thought much of children, now wanted to be a father more than anything in the world.

That he, for once in his life, didn't know what to do.

Colleen morphed into caretaking mode, and it occurred to him, however briefly, that she needed this, too.

"I already told you that healers can't fix what's wrong with her," she said gently. "And I think you know that, too. In your own way."

He hung his head. The hand not gripping the phone pressed a fist to his forehead. "Yes."

"I don't know if you can save your marriage, Aggie. Do you think you can?"

The hesitation before he answered was more an answer than the words that came next. "No."

"But that's not what you're trying to save anymore, is it?"

"No."

"No," she repeated. "You're trying to save your daughter. And you will."

Augustus' voice cracked when he asked, "How?"

"You need to have her committed. Not only for your daughter's sake, but hers." Colleen didn't hesitate. She didn't sugarcoat. This was what he needed, and he now understood, why it was always her he intended to call. "She's a danger to herself, and the baby. And if you don't do this, if you don't commit her, then Christmas this year is likely going to be hard for another reason."

"You're right. I know you're right."

"I wish to God I wasn't," she said, sighing. "I'll be home for Christmas this year, Aggie. I'll be there when she's born, and I'll do whatever I can to help."

"You'll be home? Evangeline said—"

"I know what Evangeline said," Colleen said. "She... she isn't wrong. But I don't need seclusion. I need my family. And... sounds like they need me."

Augustus felt like crying, but found he didn't need to now. A new, decisive resolve had overcome him, one that was more comforting than any words. He knew now what he needed to do, and in the knowing was peace. He'd always known, but knowing was a process.

"We do need you, Colleen," he said.

CHAPTER 15

Now, Here We Are

Colleen had never been more relieved for a school term to end.

Winter term would pick up after Christmas, and she had over a month to herself before the bustle of school could keep her mind busy. University was a much needed distraction, but it was also a terribly potent reminder, and every time her studying produced no clarity, or her assignments didn't get top marks, Colleen was further aware that control was as elusive as love.

She saw Noah twice in passing since the night in the library where she'd found his father's letter, but if he saw her, he gave no indication. He never called or wrote to ask after "Madeline," or express annoyance that she'd read his letter, which was clear by the haphazard way she'd left it. More likely, he was wondering why the hell she couldn't just move on.

Colleen *had* moved on, as much as she could, with her heart still so sore. She didn't harbor any fantasies of Noah coming to his senses and landing on her doorstop. But moving on wasn't the same as being okay.

She wasn't due home for the holidays for another three weeks, and it would be a very long three weeks if she couldn't find ways to occupy herself.

Augustus' call had reinvigorated her. Colleen hated to see him in pain, *especially* him, because he was already impossibly hard on himself when he didn't live up to his own exacting standards. Augustus was a good man who'd tried to be a good husband, but picked the wrong wife to practice on. Colleen stayed out of things until now, but she'd be damned if Ekatherina pulled her brother down into the same dark pool she was determined to drown in.

She was relieved to hear Augustus followed her advice, even if he'd only taken it halfway. He couldn't find it in himself to take his wife to an actual medical facility, so he'd hired round the clock trained caregivers, giving both him and Elizabeth relief. They'd be there until the baby was born, and then if Ekatherina showed no signs of improvement, she *would* be taken away, so as not to cause further harm to her daughter in a phase that was so important to her development.

Colleen prayed it didn't come to that, for Augustus' sake. He wasn't handling this well. He'd found an escape that proved healthy for him after Maddy's death, burying himself in building his business, but there was no escaping this. His love for Ekatherina hadn't waned with her insanity, and Colleen sensed his fear wasn't just for his unborn daughter. Maybe Ekatherina was a witch herself, because there was no other explanation for the complete spell she'd placed Augustus under, before he even stood a chance of defending himself.

Colleen struggled picturing Augustus as a father. He'd give his daughter the world, but he'd always shied away from anything resembling nurturing. He'd defended himself wholly against the everyday troubles plaguing the family, only opening himself up for Maddy. But he'd have a lot of support, that was for sure, and being able to raise his little girl alongside Olivia and Nicolas would go a long way.

Three babies, in one year. She still had trouble wrapping her mind around it.

Colleen rushed to the bathroom, hand over her mouth, and retched in the toilet.

. . .

THE CALL FROM OPHELIA CAME AROUND SUPPER THAT evening. Ophelia must have been just waking for the day back in New Orleans.

"Are we now coming to your special realization?" her great-aunt asked.

Colleen stared at the wall, nursing a cuppa from the mug she'd bought Noah that said, *Farewell, boiling water. You will be mist.* They'd both laughed for a solid ten minutes when she brought it home from the little shop on the Royal Mile where they'd bought a lot of little trinkets for her apartment.

"I don't know how to answer that."

"Oh, bless, Colleen. You do. If your determination was as strong as your denial, I daresay we wouldn't even be talking right now."

"What does that mean?"

"It means you only need me right now because of your stubborn willful disregard of reality."

Colleen scoffed. The cup burned her palms, but she liked the sensation.

"True or false. The phone was or was not already in your lap when I called?"

"Don't you ever get tired of seeing *everything*?" Colleen sighed. "Must get confusing living in two different worlds all the time."

"Infuriating, where your future is concerned."

Colleen rolled her eyes as dusk settled over the room. She'd turned the lights off, and now the exterior light was fading into the horizon. "Who should start then?"

"It's your dilemma."

"Dilemma? Is that what this is?"

"For most, it would be the cause of joy. But as we are both oh, so painfully aware, Colleen, joy is something you've never allowed yourself."

"That's not fair. Or true. I had joy with Noah." Colleen twisted the phone cord around her wrist, winding and winding.

"You could have joy again, and soon, but I need to hear you say it. Dancing around the truth is exhausting for anyone, but especially me." Ophelia erupted in a coughing fit that lasted almost a full minute. Colleen heard her spit something into a handkerchief.

Hearing her great-aunt in such decline made Colleen change her mind. She'd come home right away. She'd been so consumed with her own world that the one back home was much changed.

Colleen tried to say the words aloud, but they caught in the back of her throat. "Saying it makes this real, Tante."

"It already *is* real, darling girl, unless you plan to feign surprise in the spring?"

"I'm pregnant." The words spilled out in the middle of Ophelia's, hiding behind them.

"I should say so," Ophelia replied. "Now we're in business. Truly, I suspected it might take you another thirty minutes, and by then I'd be inclined to pick this back up tomorrow."

Colleen ignored the slight. She deserved it. Ophelia was right. "It's my own fault. I knew I needed a new diaphragm, and I should've prioritized getting into a local doctor, but... I don't know, we were happy, so if an accident happened, so what? I wasn't sure at first. I thought stress might have been the culprit. Wouldn't be the first time worrying made me tired and nauseated."

"Won't be the last, either." Ophelia cleared another productive bout of phlegm from her throat. "I'd ask if you've shared the wonderful news with the father, but we both know you have not."

"How can I tell him? He wants nothing to do with me."

"A baby changes everything."

"I will *not* lure him back to me with a child."

"Who said anything about luring? Doesn't he deserve to know?"

"If he doesn't want to marry a witch, do you really think he wants to father one?" Colleen released the phone cord and began the process of winding again. "His own dad abandoned his wife and three daughters over it."

"Mm," Ophelia replied. "Time softens all men. You saw the letter from the elder Jameson proving this is already so."

"Really, how *do* you deal with seeing every little thing?" Colleen shook her head. "Doesn't matter. He read that letter from his father and still never called. Noah's made up his mind. His prejudices outrank everything else."

"You don't know that, Colleen."

"Oh, I think I do know that! He hasn't called! He hasn't dropped by! He hasn't left me a note!"

"Nor have you."

"I've called," she defended.

"In the beginning. When both your blood was hot."

"Did you call to scold me, or to help me?"

"I am helping you." Ophelia's voice muffled as she set the phone aside and asked Aria to refill her tea.

"He's the one who left, Tante." The words were a knife to her chest, as much as coming home to her apartment devoid of his belongings had been. "He left me."

"He left a foolish fear," Ophelia corrected. "His reasons no longer matter. Your feelings about his abandoning you come secondary to what you must do now."

"I've decided to come home tomorrow."

"Oh? When did you decide this?"

Colleen grinned in spite of herself. "What, something you *didn't* already know about, old woman?"

"Old woman!" Ophelia made a *pfft* noise. "I can still wipe my own ass and drive my own cars, thank you."

"I decided just now," Colleen confessed. "I've been away too long, and no, I don't need your assessment as to *why*. I know why. I might be stubborn, but I'm not entirely lacking in self-awareness."

"I know you're not," Ophelia said. "I give you hell because you are my greatest joy, Colleen. One day, you'll be doling out advice from my seat, and I hope you'll find your own style and manner of ushering the family through their dark times."

"You have more faith in me than I'll ever have in myself."

"Your faith is failing you now because you're human," Ophelia said. "There will always be times in your life where you need your own counsel, and others where you need the comfort of others. Always trust your instincts, Colleen. They do misfire from time to time, but they are generally always more correct than our fears, or our insecurities."

"Knowing the difference is hard."

"Wisdom is fickle," Ophelia replied. "Please do come see me before Christmas, Colleen. Will you do that?"

"Of course, Tante." Colleen had the sudden, inexplicable urge to cry. "Of course I will."

The line went dead without the exchange of goodbyes, in traditional Ophelia fashion.

Colleen sat alone in the dark, staring at the thin line of orange over the hills in the distance.

Her hand hovered in midair, unsure, before she let it rest on her belly.

Life within her.

I don't want children. I have my reasons. Said to Rory. To Philip. To Noah. To anyone who would listen.

"Reasons," Colleen whispered, as the horizonal glow in the world beyond fell to darkness.

INSTINCT BROUGHT COLLEEN TO THE LIBRARY. THE TAXI, loaded with her bags, awaited outside. Her flight left in two hours, and she didn't have time to waste. She couldn't step on the plane without this closure, though. The end had been too ambiguous and one-sided. She had her own words to say, even if she wasn't ready to say any of them.

He was there, of course, sitting at the desk that told the world of his accomplishments. Oh, how she'd wanted to say, so many times, how proud she was of him. That chance would never come.

Noah didn't look up until she was standing in front of him.

"Don't say anything," Colleen said. "You already spoke your piece, and I deserve the right to say mine, even if it is months later."

Noah nodded. He dropped his pen and slipped his hands under the table. She didn't have time to analyze why. She had things to say, and only limited courage with which to say them.

"Yes, Noah Jameson, I'm a *witch.* I don't boil toads or make love potions for bored women, but I do heal. Yours isn't the first life I've saved, and it won't be the last. I won't apologize for saving you, or for being who I am. You're the one who told me I never should. It was a lesson I needed to learn, even if you didn't really mean the words."

He cringed but remained silent.

"I don't know anything about your mother, or what she could do or has done, but I'll bet she loved you with all her heart. I could've let you die out there, and you would've gone from this world believing I was exactly who you wanted me to be. But if you'd died, Noah, I would've been lost along with you. I'd do what I did again a thousand times over, because I'd rather live in a world where you were alive and full of loathing for me than one where you no longer existed."

Noah clutched both hands tightly under the table. His biceps clenched under his sweater, and he swayed lightly in his seat. He looked ready to say something, but the words never came.

Colleen slipped her hand into her tan jacket. When she opened it, the dried heather band sat on her palm. She extended her fingers and it fell to the table in a gentle tumble. "I hope one day you find the world to be as neatly tied as you desire it to be," she said, pausing only briefly to regard him one last time before slipping away.

WINTER 1975

VACHERIE, LOUISIANA
NEW ORLEANS, LOUISIANA
EDINBURGH, SCOTLAND

CHAPTER 16

Highs and Lows

Lisette showed him the trick. Nicolas was getting heavier, though not *too* heavy, of course, Charles wasn't a pussy. But it did leave him with the irrational fear that his son was going to flip out of his arms, and even though Lisette assured him that would *not* happen, he couldn't get it out of his head.

Catherine could have assured him, too, probably, but Charles, for some reason, didn't like to talk about Nicolas with her. He still returned to her each night, but the retreat from his son began to feel more like a duty than a desire. Time had run out for this cycle of whatever it was they were together, but he hadn't found the words to make it official.

Nicolas was swaddled to his chest, facing forward. He kicked his feet and giggled with delight. Charles' heart skipped. This never got old.

He trekked them around the grounds of Ophélie, reciting all the histories he remembered. Nicolas wouldn't recall any of this, but Charles didn't mind if they had to do it a hundred times. This was his boy, and he'd do right by him.

"Those parterre gardens came up with the house," he said, pointing to the right and left sides of the house. "No special story there that I know of. But the, uh, one in the back was built for our ancestor, Brigitte, and that's why they call it Brigitte's garden." He didn't add that Brigitte died there, when she flung herself to the flagstones in agony after her daughter was murdered.

Nicolas bounced on his chest.

He pointed to the second floor and Nicolas' gaze followed. "See all that ironwork in the balconies? We imported it all from Spain. That was the thing to do, I guess. All kinds of crap here was imported from Europe, and New England. I think only the cypress is from around here. Pulled from the swamp, I'd guess. And that little thing on top of the house, which looks like another little house, but has a little walkout with a view? They call that bullshit a belvedere, though I have no fucking clue why." He winced. "Sorry, Nicky. Old habit."

It would be a miracle if Nicolas didn't grow up with a mouth dirtier than a Mississippi sailor. Charles understood now why people said parenting was hard!

"Anyway, as I was saying. There were over two hundred buildings on the property before the War of Northern Aggression. Funny, right? That's what some people around here still call it. Your relatives were smart enough to make friends with the Yankees, though, son, and that's why Ophélie withstood the war." He frowned, squinting against the noonday sun. "I don't know why we tore a bunch of the buildings down, though."

Charles stepped farther away from the house and pointed out the kitchens, the old pigeonnier, the sugar mill, and blacksmith shop. He didn't really know what to say about the slave cabins. Bad things happened there, and though times had changed, bad things still happened to people with darker skin. Covering up that part of his family's past didn't make it any better, but he didn't know if it was his story to tell properly.

"I suppose you'll learn like the rest of us did that people aren't the fucking greatest, little man," Charles said, and this time didn't apologize for his use of language.

"Hey! Huck!"

Charles spun around, nearly slipping in the damp grass. In the distance, he saw Colin, jogging toward him from the direction of the house. He waved.

"Colin? What's happening?"

Colin's face immediately dissolved into what Charles thought of on himself as "daddy face." He dropped himself lower and tickled Nicolas' flushed baby cheeks. "Hey, Nic! You're growing up so fast!"

"I sure am, Uncle Colin!" Charles cried out in his best singsong baby voice.

Colin wrinkled his lips, brows knit as he stood up. "Wow, and he's already talking."

"That's my boy."

"I like what you've got going on here. He looks comfortable."

Charles adjusted his baby pack in response. "Great for both of us. I could go all day without my back screaming at me."

Colin grinned. "Listen to us, hardly twenty-five and already complaining about our backs."

"So, what's going on? Didn't know you were coming out."

"Did I interrupt something?"

Yes. "No, man, what's up?"

Colin's façade of happiness crumbled in an instant. Tears welled in his eyes. "It's almost Christmas, Huck. She's not home yet."

A jolt of ice passed through Charles' veins. Over the years he'd always held onto guilt for his trysts with Catherine, but his love for her always won out. He couldn't pinpoint exactly what had changed, though he could name a hundred things if there was one thing. Something very fundamental in the thread weaving their lives together had snapped. And now, as he looked at his oldest friend cycling through grief and confusion, he only knew guilt.

There was no *give her time* or *it'll get better* to be said. Time had passed, and nothing was better for Catherine. She'd been hinting at wanting a divorce—a divorce and remarriage to Charles. She'd dipped her toes into the conversation, feeling Charles out, and he'd managed not to encourage her too much. He was two men with Catherine now: Pre-Nicolas and Post-Nicolas, and only the version of himself prior to becoming a father would even entertain the idea.

This new man couldn't, and even thinking of creating that much chaos in his life left him feeling ill.

"I'm sorry," Charles said. He tried to swallow the thickness out of his throat.

"What am I supposed to do?" Colin leaned against the side of a barn. This one was in such disrepair now that it needed to be scrapped for parts. Charles wondered why this hadn't happened yet, then realized it was probably his call. No one would dare alter anything at Ophélie without his blessing.

"What can you do?" Charles asked. He shouldn't be the one on the other end of these questions, but he was the *only* one who could be, because Colin didn't have any other friends. He'd never had more than acquaintances, even when they were boys. Their relationship was orchestrated by their fathers, which might have been the only reason it survived so long. Friendships weren't important to him, because he always had something more pressing to deal with, like his grades, or getting into college. Colin never saw the sad irony in how hard he worked to create a life for himself while never actually living.

"That's what I'm asking myself, Huck. I don't *know* what to do. For the first time in my life, I have no direction. I'm... I'm aimless! I'm wandering the desert, lost." Colin leaned his head into the rotting wood. "She's left before, but she's always come back. This time is different."

"What about Oz?" Catherine liked to sound gracious about how she'd leave her son at Colin's mother's house for a few hours for visitation, but Charles knew, as only a father could, that these dangling carrots were torture, and sometimes he hated her for being so cruel to Colin and using their son as a device.

Colin shrugged. "She lets me see him, but she's never there. He's too young to understand, but someday..." He glanced up and looked directly at Charles. "I remember you telling me how hard it was for you to grow up without a father. Without presence from both parents. I don't want that for Oz."

"And that, my friend, is why Cordelia isn't on the street."

Colin pointed at the house. "She's not here, though."

"It was for the best."

"Maybe she didn't want to watch you with Lisette."

"That would imply that Cordelia has a heart. She does not."

Colin didn't argue. His worn, haggard face showed his surrender. "I just want her *home,* Huck." His face fell and he whipped his hands up to hide the betrayal of emotion. Charles watched, helpless, racked with guilt, as his best friend sobbed quietly and alone.

Charles tangled Nicolas' fingers in his, thinking.

He could fix this.

He, and maybe he alone.

Catherine would live in this limbo as long as Charles allowed their sad game of house to continue. And why had he? It wasn't for himself—not this time. For her, perhaps, and some old, powerful love still living in his heart. He couldn't reconcile the way he still loved her so deeply but no longer needed her. There was no chance of loving anyone again the way he'd loved Catherine Connelly. None. But nor did he need that in his life now that he knew the true, pure love of becoming a father.

"Want me to talk to her?"

Colin wiped his eyes with the back of his hands. Already, he was coming back together, reassembling himself into the cool, collected lawyer he'd spent his life becoming. "You?"

"Maybe it would help... I don't know. I don't know why I said it."

Colin's glimmering eyes brightened. "No... no, you might be on to something. She's always liked you, Huck. You know she's the reason I stopped being so mad at you, after the whole college thing?"

I know more about Catherine than you ever will. "You don't say?"

"That's the beauty of Catherine. She sees the best in everyone." He looked away and exhaled a jagged breath. "Except me, I guess."

"She knows who you are," Charles said. "Do you?"

"What does that mean?"

I can't fucking believe I'm about to save the marriage of the only woman I've ever loved. "Come on, Colin. I've spent my whole life listening to your bullshit judgments of me, but have you ever, even fucking *once,* looked at your own self?"

Colin recoiled. "Nicolas is going to grow up with a filthy sailor's mouth. You know that, don't you?"

"There are worse problems to have," Charles said. "Right now, you have a worse problem. Unless you can start looking at yourself through more honest eyes, it's going to stay a problem."

Colin shuffled his feet, eyes cast into the dirt.

"You said Cat sees the best in everyone. But did you ever think that maybe she wants someone to feel that way about her?"

"I do!"

Charles shook his head. "Do you?"

"I don't know where you're going with this."

"How many times have you described Cat using words like *dreamer* or *idealist*? You know those are just fancy words for being a fucking flight risk, right? For being less than?"

"That's not fair. I love those things about my wife."

"Love, or tolerate?"

"You really have an opinion about this, don't you?"

"You worried more about my opinion, or your wife's?"

Colin grunted and paced the ground around the side of the barn. "I've always known who Catherine was."

"Listen to yourself!" Charles cried, then immediately kissed and soothed his son in apology. "Didn't mean to yell, buddy." He returned his focus to Colin. "You talk about her like you made a concession with her. Like you fucking settled! You don't think she knows that's how you feel about her?"

"Then what do you suggest? Since you're an expert?"

"You do the same thing to me," Charles said, lowering his voice. The words were painful to say, as painful as the mirror Colin always held up for those he didn't approve of. "All my life I've known I can never be the man you think I should be. So, I stopped trying."

"Huck—"

"So, you want to know why your wife isn't home for Christmas? She stopped trying, too." Charles clapped a hand on Colin's back. His heart ached, and he didn't want to be here anymore. "If you want her to start, then jump down off that fucking pedestal you like to live on, wipe the blood off your nose, and be a human being."

COLLEEN WAS HOME, BUT NOT REALLY.

Ophelia didn't question when she said she wanted to stay at The Gardens for this visit, nor did she chide Colleen when she didn't immediately tell her mother and siblings she was back. Perhaps Ophelia had seen this future. Perhaps she had a deeper sense of Colleen's angst and understood it needed to unravel in phases.

Whatever reasons initially propelled her to hide in isolation, among the cavernous halls and colorful gardens of the Deschanel family center, she now had another reason for staying.

In the year Colleen had been away, Ophelia had become an old woman.

Ophelia Deschanel had been old Colleen's entire life. She'd never had the honor of knowing the younger woman who'd stood up to a whole line of heirs; who'd forsaken romantic love for familial. Who'd sacrificed everything to save the family when it appeared nothing could.

Ophelia was the glue, and without her, Colleen feared the whole thing would come toppling down around them.

Her aunt now rose later in the mornings and retired earlier in the evenings. She took her tea inside, because the heat, even in the winter, was too much for her withering constitution. She'd canceled the last three quarterly Council meetings, which at first Colleen was relieved about, seeing as she had no desire to come home, but now understood wasn't for her benefit at all.

Ophelia was dying. Really, truly, actually dying now.

Aria interrupted her reverie to announce Colleen had a phone call. She pulled herself together and went into the women's parlor to answer it. Before she lifted the phone, though, she froze. If someone was calling her at The Gardens, then they knew she was back in New Orleans.

There was only one way to find out. “Colleen speaking.”

“Colleen!”

Colleen recognized the voice, but couldn’t place it, not right away. The agony underscoring the sound of her own name, the desperation, rooted her to her seat. Something was wrong.

Very wrong.

“Catherine,” she said, finally, as the recollection came to her. “I’m sorry, this just caught me off guard. I didn’t expect your call. Or anyone’s, for that matter.”

“Huck told me you were home.”

“My brother knows?”

“He knows everything, Colleen. Don’t ask me how. I’m not sure I want to know.”

God, I hope the fool hasn’t told Mama yet. “I’d appreciate if you kept that to yourself for now. I’ll be going to see my mother in a couple days, but for now I need some time with my aunt.”

“Of course. I won’t say a word.” There was a sharp edge, like a boulder teetering on the brink. Catherine was the boulder, but what wasn’t immediately clear was the distance to the edge.

“Something is wrong,” Colleen noted, jumping right into it before Catherine could demure. She thought of her own conversation with Ophelia a week back, where she was the Catherine in that scenario. She understood herself, and Ophelia, better now.

“Very wrong,” Catherine said, and the sigh that came next sounded almost relieved. “So wrong, I don’t know how to make it right.”

“There’s always a way to make things right,” Colleen said, even though she didn’t quite believe the words. “Is it Huck?”

Catherine dissolved into a fresh batch of tears. “Isn’t it always?”

Colleen’s heart leapt forward. “Colin knows.”

“Heavens to God, no! If he knew…”

“Then, what is it?” For a brief, horrific moment, Colleen actually wondered if her brother was capable of violence against a woman. He wasn't. There was no way. She refused to believe that.

"It's over between us. Huck and me. He… it was his choice. I don't want to get into it."

"That's okay. I don't need the details." Colleen paused. "How long, though? How long were you having an affair?"

"Affair." Catherine coughed out the word, expelling it like poison. "When you say it like that, it sounds so terrible."

"You're a married woman, Catherine. That's what it is."

"Not anymore," Catherine said. "Since fall, I guess. A few months. Does it matter?"

"Does it? You called me for a reason. You could have called anyone else."

"No, I couldn't have," Catherine said. "My mother would disown me. I have no friends, and Huck… no, he can't ever know. I mean *ever*, Colleen."

"I still don't know what we're talking about."

"I'm pregnant!" Catherine cried out, laughing, as if it were obvious.

Maybe it was her own inopportune circumstances, but Colleen was completely taken aback by the revelation. "And you think it's Charles'?"

"It *is* his baby, Colleen. I haven't been with Colin in half a year. We stopped having sex long before I found my way back to your brother, so there's no way to even *pretend* this baby is a Sullivan."

Catherine, pregnant, with another Deschanel child. Perhaps a second heir. Married to another man, in love with one she couldn't have. What a terrible mess.

"Cat, there are places—"

"No," Catherine asserted. "Not that. That isn't an option for me."

"Okay," Colleen said. "What, then, would you like to do? You can't think breaking up two marriages is the answer. If you did, you would've done that without tracking me down."

"I'm having this, baby, Colleen, but it doesn't mean I have to be the one to raise it."

Colleen fell back in her chair. "Did you have someone in mind?"

"No," Catherine said. "But if anyone can solve this problem, I know in my heart it's you."

CHAPTER 17

The Ghosts are Gone

Charles finally told Maureen to stop fussing, after the hundredth time she'd sprung forward to smooth out the blanket Nicolas and Olivia were lying on.

"Jesus, can you be less neurotic?"

"There's dust on the wood floor!"

"What house are we in again?"

Maureen lowered her voice. "Even Mama isn't *perfect* at cleanliness."

"I heard that!" Irish Colleen called as she carried a tray of snacks into the parlor. She winced as she knelt to settle it on the coffee table.

"Let me help with that, Mama," Charles said, starting to get up.

"Nonsense," she chided and maneuvered herself to block his assistance. "You treat me like I'm old, when I'm hardly forty!"

"Forty-three," Charles replied.

"As I said." Irish Colleen ran her hands down her apron and surveyed her handiwork. "There. Eat." She turned to leave, when a thought passed over her. "You know your father would be seventy this year. God rest his soul."

Maureen's breath hitched. *Daddy.* She and Charles exchanged a look, but he didn't know how things had changed for her.

When her mother was gone, back to the kitchen to tend to whatever busy work kept her occupied these days, Maureen breathed out a sigh that ended in a soft sob.

"What's wrong?"

"The ghosts are gone, Huck."

"What do you mean, the ghosts are gone?"

She trained a hard look on him. "You know exactly what I mean. The ghosts. Are gone."

"Dad?"

"Dad, Maddy, that rapist from my middle school whom I won't speak about in front of my daughter. All our ancestors. All of them."

"Since when?"

Maureen crawled over to Olivia, who was blinking rapidly to expel something from her eye. She exhaled in relief to see it was only a fiber from the blanket, and flicked it aside. "Since I moved in with Edouard."

"They've been gone that long? And you're just now telling me?"

She shot him a glare over her shoulder. "Don't get self-righteous with me, after what you and Augustus did. Not now or ever."

Charles joined her on the blanket. He stretched out next to Nicolas, and the infant curled into his father's side. He was a natural father, and Maureen marveled at the dramatic change that had overcome her brother in recent months.

"They haven't been back at all?"

Maureen took some wet naps from her diaper bag and dapped at the corner of Olivia's mouth. She'd missed some crusted milk from the earlier feeding. "No, and I don't expect they ever will be."

"Why do you think they left?"

She shrugged. "Who knows?"

"You must have a theory at least."

"Well..." Maureen inhaled a sharp breath. "I first thought maybe it was my pregnancy, but I've been pregnant before, and the ghosts were just as annoying as they'd always been. *Then*, I thought it was turning eighteen, but they were still there for a few months, you know? So the only thing I can figure is my marriage. Or the Blanchard House. Or maybe both. Without someone who knows anything about it, all I can do is guess."

"Ophelia might know."

Maureen laughed. "That old coot?"

"She knows more than anyone else about what we are."

"What's done is done, Huck. There's no bringing them back even if we do get answers. Don't ask me how I know that, I just do. And I pray to God Olivia doesn't suffer the way I did."

Charles rolled onto his back. "I wish I'd known that. There were things I wanted to say to Dad."

"Keep your voice down!"

"Sorry. Jeez." Closer to a whisper, he asked, "Did he ever say anything about me?"

Maureen started to roll her eyes, only to realize the cruelty felt foreign to her now. She didn't want to hurt her brother. Or anyone. Not anymore. "He didn't have free rein of the place, so I don't think he knew about... well, all the stuff you were up to, if that's what you're asking. He said he was proud of you, and loved you, but words are words. He was bound to me, and bound to the house, and more specifically, only in places where I *was* in the house, so his world was limited." She tucked the soiled rag in a side pocket. "I like to think that he was looking after me until that duty passed to my husband, and then he went on to a better place."

Charles wrinkled his face into a frown as he processed this. "Yeah, but that doesn't explain why the others left, too."

"No," Maureen agreed, wishing now that she'd never brought the topic up. "It doesn't. And speculating doesn't do a damn thing to help."

"I'm sorry," Charles said abruptly.

"Sorry?"

"For everything, Maureen. I never wanted to make your life harder. I made the choice I thought would be best for you, but I see now it wasn't my choice to make."

Maureen pretended to organize her bag so he wouldn't see the tears tickling her eyes. "Things worked out just as they should have."

"I can't stop thinking about what you told me, about your hus—"

"Not in front of Olivia," she hissed. "I'm trying to make our house a home. For her."

Maureen told him about her plans to persuade Edouard to soften his heart and welcome her in. She would need to make sacrifices, too, she said, because Edouard was not the least bit attractive and she could never forget what he did to her, even if she had done a fair job pressing it into the recesses of her memory bank. But if she could forgive that, then he could learn to accept that this was his life, now, and he had a wife and daughter who looked forward to seeing him every day.

"I can make him love me," she finished. "If anyone can, it's me."

The sad, pitying look on her brother's face wounded her. She wished she hadn't seen it.

"You could divorce him," Charles offered. "You don't need his money, and you and Olivia already have his name. We could make it happen without hurting your reputation."

"Nonsense," Maureen countered, disappearing back into the tightly woven world of fantasy she'd created in order to survive, just as she'd always done.

ELIZABETH COLLAPSED ON HER BED, LETTING THE weight of the world roll off and onto the floor.

The past months had been filled with their share of long days, but today was the culmination of all of them, where her emotional capacity waved the white flag.

Today wasn't special. Ekatherina went into labor, sure, but that was easy compared to taking care of her. Even after Augustus hired the white coats to mind her, Elizabeth couldn't sleep easy leaving her to men who were only paid to care, so she stayed on. Ekatherina seemed to appreciate it, or at least understood that enemy was a sliding scale. Elizabeth was an angel of mercy when compared to the psychiatric task force that had moved into Magnolia Grace.

You stay. They go. Ekatherina pouted after the first day.

I'll stay if you want, but I have no say over them being here.

He hate me.

Aggie? Nah, if he hated you, he would've had you committed to an asylum. This here is a mercy.

Maureen was more helpful than Elizabeth imagined she'd be, and she supposed motherhood had changed her wayward sister. Maureen jumped in like a freshly enlisted nurse in the war, rolling up her sleeves and never complaining. Elizabeth couldn't tell her all of it... she would never, ever tell anyone about the banister incident, or the one the real nurses later caught, with the knife. Those stories belonged to the couple living at Magnolia Grace only; Elizabeth, just a bystander. The only thing that would make all this harder on Augustus was if everyone knew the details.

Her calls to Connor remained unanswered. She tried to tell herself Rory was just bad at passing along messages, but her heart knew better. Vanessa had probably never touched drugs of any kind, let alone cocaine. She was pristine and pure, unmarred by visions or emotional outbursts, or the cynicism of life.

Elizabeth didn't know why today was the day it all came flooding forth, spilling over the surface of her defenses, and she didn't care.

She only knew she was done.

When she awoke, the sun had finished setting. Her room was bathed in darkness. She wasn't alone.

Elizabeth rolled to her side. Connor's dark eyes flashed in the ambient moonlight.

She blinked hard.

"Lizzy." His voice was hoarse. How long had he been there?

"You came all this way to break up with me," she said. Without realizing it, she drew her arms up in a defensive pose.

"What? Break up with you?" He narrowed the gap between them on the bed, inching closer, even as she drew away. "Why would you think that?"

"Vanessa," she accused.

He recoiled. "Vanessa? Who on earth is Vanessa?"

"If you didn't want me to know about her, you should've told Rory not to open his big mouth."

Connor set his hand on her hip. He let it move up, over her waist, but something made him think better of it. "Wait, you're serious?"

She rolled away from him. "This isn't funny! Just tell me the truth already! I'm so goddamn tired... I've stayed clean, God knows how, and I saved my sister-in-law's life, and I'm just *done* and I need you to be honest with me so we can get this over with!"

"Lizzy..." Connor sighed. "I'm so confused. I want to be honest with you, but I don't know what's going on."

"I guess I'm not the dead wife in your future after all."

Connor went stiff at her side. His hand fell away. "That's not funny."

"The dead wife part, or it not being me?"

"None of it," he said. "I don't know who Vanessa is, and I don't know why you'd think I came home to *break up* with you. Elizabeth, *I love you.*" He reached for her arm and gently tugged her, rolling her back in his direction. "I left so many messages for you."

"Where?"

"On your answering machine."

"On my..." Elizabeth laughed. She couldn't help it. Charles bought the cursed thing for Irish Colleen, who plugged it in and then acted like it didn't exist. "What about the messages I left for you?"

"Carolina gave them to me last week. She found the pile on Rory's desk. I was rarely home in Boston, to be honest. If I wasn't at school, I was hanging with my friend Van..." Connor's words trailed off to laughter. "Van. Vanessa. Goddamn, Rory never listened to me!"

"Your friend was Van?"

"Yes, Van. A dude. He had that game everyone's playing at the arcade, you know, Pong. Except his mom is rich and bought him one for home. We played that every night until we dropped, and every weekend, too. Shit's addicting."

"Pong," Elizabeth repeated.

"Holy shit, Lizzy. All this time you thought I wasn't calling you because I was with another girl?"

Elizabeth sighed, turning away again, her sore heart growing more tender with what now seemed like utter foolishness.

"And here I thought you were too busy for me." Connor shook his head. "I wasn't mad or anything. I knew you were helping your brother. But I missed you so much, and when your mother called me—"

"Mama called you?"

"She called and said you needed me. She said... it went against her better judgment, but if it was okay with my parents, I could stay here, at the house. In a guest bedroom, of course. They agreed, because it meant I could come visit my mom in the hospital, too, and so... here I am."

"I did need you," she conceded, but couldn't make herself turn around to face him. She wondered how Irish Colleen had the insight into her frame of mind to make this call, and realized her mother often had unique ways of surprising her.

"Did?"

Silence permeated the dusky room. "Do," she said, exhaling a breath she felt she'd held for months. A breath that had been a shield from the pain, both her own and all she'd been absorbing for others.

Connor curled up behind her, settling himself into the bends of her body. "There's only you, Lizzy. There's only ever been you. There'll only ever be you. Just you."

The last of the bricks holding back the well of Elizabeth's emotions crumbled, and she sobbed as he held her, and she let him, because nothing could harm her now that his touch couldn't solve.

CHAPTER 18

Christmas Eve

Evangeline hadn't known how much she missed her sister until Colleen climbed into the bed with her, just as they'd done years ago, when they were girls and not women.

Being home was odd, with a hazy, abstract quality, as if she'd stepped back into a world that wasn't quite hers, but was close. She took this as a sign she wasn't done healing, and that being away was still for the best. But when her heart didn't explode, she knew this was also a sign, one that told her it was okay to come home every now and then, too.

Christmas at Ophélie held a magic all on its own. The staircases spiraled with lighted holly, and the entire property smelled of warm gingerbread. In the study, the tree reached as tall as the high tray ceiling, presents overflowing nearly into the hall.

The memory of Maddy was dimmest here, for they'd treated Ophélie as a summer home only, until after she died and Mama had the idea that the family estate was where they needed to be to heal. Her ghost was everywhere anyway, no matter where they were on Christmas Eve, because this would always and forever be Maddy's day. She'd unintentionally sealed her name on all future December 24ths and there was nothing to be done about it.

This year was different, though, because instead of only

mourning lost life, they were celebrating the advent of new. Olivia, Nicolas, and soon, at any moment, Augustus' daughter would enter the world. They brought Ekatherina to Ophélie and created a birthing suite, so that the family could stay close to her progress without driving an hour back and forth into town. Her earlier labor had been a false one, but the doctor insisted the real one would be imminent. Augustus' drawn, pale face broke Evangeline in a new way; the way only being horribly right about something horribly wrong could. No matter how much she'd disliked Ekatherina, she'd never wanted their marriage to come to this hostile cease-fire of cold looks and whispered curses.

But there would be a fourth child born soon, now. Colleen's.

Colleen, who never wanted children, now had to find the courage to do so.

And they'd get to that subject, they would.

But first, Evangeline had something to get off her chest, to the only person she could ever say the words to.

"I met someone, too," she said, as Colleen settled herself under the blankets.

"I figured you had. It's why you left, isn't it?"

"Not the main reason," Evangeline replied. "Only the last one."

"Why didn't you tell me?"

Evangeline rolled her face to the ceiling. "I didn't know why, at first. I tried to, but the words never came, and I stopped trying to force them. The more complicated my feelings got for Amnesty, the harder they were for me to understand, let alone try to explain them to you."

"Amnesty." Colleen let the word roll off her tongue softly. "What a lovely name." No acknowledgement of Evangeline's lover being a woman, and with that exclusion, no judgment, either.

Evangeline told her older sister about the night she met Amnesty, and every night after. About the friendship she refused to define until it defined itself, and she lost her heart in the process. She didn't leave out a single detail, because this was more to Evangeline than sharing with Colleen; it was an unburdening. With the story out, with someone else in the universe possessed of the facts, they no longer needed to possess her.

"I'm so sorry, Evie." Colleen laced their hands together under the blanket. "Our family has been targeted by many people with evil in their hearts, this... this is shocking, even to me."

"I think she did love me, Colleen. That's the thing. She did. I know she did."

"I'm not talking about Amnesty, I mean her father. It's hard to blame her for wanting to find a way to earn freedom for her and her sister. She didn't expect to have feelings for you."

Evangeline snickered. "Ten dollars says I expected it less."

"I know." Colleen released her hand and stared at the ceiling, where a hundred points of light danced across the plaster, seeping in through the pattern on the lace curtains Irish Colleen had crafted by hand, years ago. "I'd guess you're confused a bit, too."

"About?"

"Your sexuality."

Evangeline shook her head against the pillow. "No, Leena. I was. I'm not anymore."

"Are you going to tell me?" She looked at her in the dark. "You know I don't have judgment for anyone's choices, as long as they don't hurt anyone. Right? You know I love you, and that love comes in many forms."

Evangeline rolled her eyes. "If that's your way of saying you're cool with me being a lezzy, you sound more like one of those whack job psychologists that come on Mama's TV programs."

Colleen feigned offense. "That was my best attempt at being supportive, thank you very much."

"Well, I'm not a lesbian. I'm not exactly straight, either." She shrugged. "I guess I'm both?"

"Bisexual," Colleen affirmed.

"I'm a scientist, Colleen. I don't care about labels, unless they were given to peer-reviewed research."

"Oh, *excuse* me."

"Besides, I don't have any interest in dating. Not right now. I want to finish school and figure things out before I'll have any time for social norms."

"I see."

"You see," Evangeline parroted in a teasing voice.

"I get it," Colleen said. "You're so above it all."

This sent them both into a fit of laughter, first Colleen, and then Evangeline. When the giggles settled, Evangeline laid her head on Colleen's shoulder. "I do miss Aggie. I'm glad he has Lizzy."

"And a daughter soon."

"I notice you didn't mention the Russian. Any chance you finally see what I see?"

"I've seen it for a while, Evie, but Augustus is a grown man who makes his own choices. He chose her, and we don't have to understand it."

"I'll be damned if she hurts him, Leena."

"She already has."

Evangeline grimaced. "I hope he takes his daughter and throws Comrade Ekatherina out in the street."

"What would Dad say if he heard you talk like that?"

"Dad would have had the bitch deported a long time ago."

Colleen laughed. "No, I don't think so. Augustus is just like him. You don't see it? Both stubborn, men of honor. You couldn't tell Dad a damn thing, and Aggie is no different."

"She's not one of us, Colleen, and she doesn't want to be."

"Neither does Cordelia. Or Edouard."

"And Noah?" Evangeline asked gently.

Colleen turned away.

"You know you can't keep things from me," she implored. "I told you about Amnesty, which wasn't easy, even now. It still hurts."

"I know."

"We can hurt together. It wouldn't be the first time."

"There's nothing to say. Whatever love he had for me wasn't bigger than his bigotry."

"What about the letter you found? From his dad?"

"A lotta good that did." Colleen told her about their last encounter, in the library. "He's made his choice, and he's living with it. I have to now, too."

Evangeline lifted herself up on one arm, incredulous. "Colleen! This isn't a regular old breakup! He got you knocked up! You're carrying his *baby* and he doesn't just get to be a bigoted asshole anymore."

"This isn't helping me feel better."

"Is that what we're doing? I didn't realize."

Colleen nudged Evangeline back down and curled up against her chest. "Stop pretending there's a future that involves Noah. It hurts, when I know it isn't possible." She swallowed." How am I going to raise a child while I'm in medical school? Alone? I'm six months along, and I'm going to have to answer this question very soon."

"Mama would raise your baby for you, you know that... or you could always consider adoption, but it would be hard to think of a Deschanel in someone else's household, living a whole different life..."

"Lives are a gift in our family, we both know this," Colleen whispered, careful not to let her voice carry across their childhood home. "Mama raised seven of us. I wouldn't ask it of her again. She should enjoy her years as a grandmother, not be burdened by them."

Evangeline stroked her hair. "Maybe I could move to Scotland and help you."

"What about MIT?"

"What of it? I don't think the school is going anywhere."

"Stop," Colleen pleaded, turning her face away as the tears streamed down her cheek and onto her pillow. "I don't want to talk about this anymore tonight. Let's get through tomorrow, and then... I don't know. I don't know anything anymore."

"It's going to be okay," Evie assured her, followed by a soft yawn. "I promise."

Colleen kissed her fist and closed her eyes. Evangeline realized what she was doing and followed suit.

"For Maddy," they whispered together, in the darkness.

Elsewhere in the house, Ekatherina screamed as the first throes of labor washed over her.

CHAPTER 19
Christmas Day

When Colleen woke Christmas morning, Evangeline had already slipped away, likely to another guest room to catch some extra sleep before their mother called them down for breakfast. Christmas breakfast was a sacred tradition in the Deschanel household. As the years drifted by, and her children's interest in the magic of the holiday waned, Irish Colleen rose later and later on the holiday morning, but the tradition was one that would live on always.

A drone of voices carried upstairs. At least some of the family were up, then, unless it was the doctors, who'd been flurrying about the house all night. No word of Ekatherina's quickening yet, but her labor was in full swing, they said, and would prove to be a long one. Both Colleen and Evangeline tried to lay hands on her, to ease her pains, but Ekatherina chased them both out with curses hurled in Russian.

Colleen rose to gather her bearings and find her robe before a wave of nausea stole over her, and she stepped swiftly into the adjoining bathroom.

In the mirror, a stranger gazed back. Dark crescents held residence under her eyes, framed by swollen cheeks and a soul-deep tiredness. Twenty-six weeks with child and she'd managed to keep this secret through evasiveness and chunky sweaters. Only Evangeline, Ophelia, and Irish Colleen knew, but there was no hiding it anymore.

Who had she become? A woman who'd given her heart alongside her reason, setting everything she had ever admired about herself aside. Who was she, if not the sensible one? Only a third child, but nevertheless looked upon as the next leader of the family.

Colleen turned on the faucet, impatient, not waiting for the water to warm. She splashed the cold on her face, relaxing as the shock settled over her.

When she opened her robe, observing the swell of her belly, she understood the time had come for honesty. Inside, her daughter was the size of a mango, only several months from emerging into the world. Denial served no one, and Colleen was nothing if not a consummate planner.

Amelia. Don't listen to my heartache, my dearest. You're a part of me. I would give up everything for you.

Closing her robe, Colleen went to join the family and share her news.

AUGUSTUS PACED THE HALLWAY, FROM THE END HOUSING the rooms they'd turned into the birthing suite, to the other, where his sisters slept, awaiting the rise of Christmas morning.

Ekatherina had been in labor over twelve hours now, but the doctor, weary, eyes glassy, reported she was nowhere near delivery. *It could be hours. She's fighting it, and her body isn't fighting harder than she is.*

How many?

She may not deliver until tomorrow.

If that were true, Ekatherina's agony would last well over thirty-six hours. Her screams were muffled by pillows held by caring nurses, but Augustus felt every one of them, deep in his bones.

He would be there with her, if only she'd let him. He'd gladly experience as much of her pain alongside her as he could, or at least be there to absorb her rage and sadness.

No matter how Ekatherina had shoved him crudely to the sidelines of both their marriage and her pregnancy, Augustus still loved her. He would still do anything in the world for her, including take her place, God willing.

At the other end of the hall, Colleen slept, unsuspecting. Augustus prided himself on not being a meddler like many other sharing his name. The business with Maureen still plagued him, and always would. Colleen had never needed him in any meaningful way, and though she didn't ask for his help now, he trusted his instincts that she would benefit from it just the same.

He hoped.

He prayed.

Hoped he'd made the right decision. Prayed if he hadn't, that Colleen could forgive him.

CHARLES HADN'T SLEPT A WINK.

Although Lisette chided him for it, claiming it was unsafe, he gently nestled Nicolas in bed beside him, on the side of the bed that would've been Cordelia's, had their marriage been anything close to normal. Sleep was impossible, so there was no chance of him rolling over on his precious boy. If Cordelia found out, she'd be outraged, for no other reason than she loved to criticize his choices, but she slept in the garçonnière on Christmas Eve, the old detached living quarters once reserved for the young men coming of age in the family. Charles' own father, August, had lived there once upon a time. Charles never had the chance, because August insisted Ophélie was no place for children.

Maybe he was right, but Charles intended to fill the halls with them anyway.

How many? Well, as many as Lisette could bear, and she assured him the women in her family's crowning glory was their impeccable fertility.

Cordelia stayed the night to pretend their marriage was more than a sham, when there was no one staying under the roof at Ophélie who didn't know better. Charles allowed her foolishness, because it was Christmas, and if there was any time to lay aside animosity for amity, it was now.

But Cordelia wasn't the only one testing him.

Catherine was the last person he wanted to be thinking about, as he watched his son's soft, peaceful sleep, because she was only person with the power to distract him from what was most important to him now.

There's something I have to tell you, Huck. Something that can't wait.

He'd promised to meet her, and then failed to. It would've been nothing to drive into town, and listen to what she had to say, but was this not always the way of things with her? It was an endless loop, one he could never get ahead of, and never win, because of the interminable circumlocution, circling, circling, repeating a version of the past that always ended the same way and then began again.

I love you, but I can't do this. I'm sorry. Merry Christmas, Cat. He hung up before she could change his mind.

Catherine was a dream that only worked if he chose never to wake up.

Lisette was real. Flesh and blood, eager to please, ready to love and be loved. She had no visions of another life, or aspirations beyond what Charles could offer. She was his, and he thought he could be hers, too.

She wasn't Catherine, and that was the problem.

She wasn't Catherine, and that was fine by him.

Charles brushed his hand over Nicolas' fine, dark baby hair and waited for his mother to call them to breakfast, like she always had, every Christmas, except the one that had altered their lives forever.

Elizabeth kissed Connor to wake him.

"Shh," she whispered, when he stirred. "Mama will be up soon."

"Oh, shit," he murmured in confusion, running his hands over his nude belly. "I didn't mean to fall asleep in here, Lizzy."

"I know." She kissed him again. "I'm glad you did." She reached under the blanket. He was hard for her, but it was nearly six, and if Mama wasn't awake, she'd be any minute. There was no better way to ruin their living arrangement then being discovered, naked, in bed together. Besides, they had their whole lives—or as long as fate allowed her. "Now get dressed, man, and get the hell out of here."

Connor grinned through his sleepiness and saluted her.

"I love you," she called, as loudly as she dared, when he turned to blow her a kiss from the door, shuffling into his pants with a lazy hop.

MAUREEN AND EDOUARD STAYED IN THE GUEST HOUSE TO the rear of the property with Olivia. There was a room available in the Big House, but Edouard insisted he needed his quiet, which she read as a place to escape as soon as the requisite activities were over.

She couldn't complain. He'd come. They were due at his sister's house for dinner, but he'd put up no argument when she asked him to attend Christmas morning with her family. He'd made only one request, and when she asked Charles to help, he immediately put the staff to the task of fixing up the guest house, even though it hadn't been used in years. The house was so big, the family never needed to use it, but the staff kept it up just well enough.

She hoped Edouard saw how agreeable she could be; how acquiescent. *Why, yes, dear, I'm happy to have dinner with your sisters who both hate my guts. Do you mind tolerating my family for a few hours?*

It was even his idea to stay Christmas Eve night. He'd asked after hotels in the area, and she laughed and said, what, in Vacherie? Really? He didn't share her amusement, and when he'd doubled down on his desire for privacy—emphasizing that a house with a woman in active labor was far from quiet—she came up with the compromise.

He even shared a bed with her, and *that* was progress. Never mind that the guest house only had one they could ready in time for the visit.

Maureen nursed Olivia by the old fireplace, filled with a hope that was too big to be dwarfed by anything as meddlesome as reality.

Colleen heard her siblings stir in the adjoining rooms as she left hers. The rich smell of sausage and *pain perdu* wafted up from downstairs. So Mama *was* up, and very soon, the house would come to life with her.

She dipped her toe down one step and froze.

Noah stood at the bottom of the stairs.

At the sight of her belly protruding from the thin robe, his jaw hung slack, and he seemed to forget everything he'd intended to say. He fumbled the gift he held in his hands, as he snaked one out to grip the banister.

Behind him, his father, Kellan, laid an encouraging hand on his shoulder. Irish Colleen appeared and placed her hand on the other, in a strange, unexpected sign of unity.

Colleen hardly had time to make sense of any of it.

"What..." Colleen's words failed her. She reached out for purchase, afraid of losing her footing, equally unable to look away. "Noah."

"I was wrong." Noah fumbled.

Colleen's foot hovered over the next step. She withdrew it and gaped at him, wordless at his appearance and his apology. How many months had she imagined these words, before abandoning the hope?

"I was so very wrong, Colleen. I was afraid, and I let that fear take over, and once it did, I didn't know how to shake it. Not even my father could peel it back."

"No," she said. "You don't know fear until you watch the person you love most in the world dying in front of you."

Noah shuddered as he drew a breath. "I don't have words strong enough to say how sorry I am for closing my mind when you opened yours. I told you it was safe with me, and I hurt you when that promise was put to the test. Almost daily, I thought of going back to you and saying all these things, but every day that passed made that feel more and more impossible, because every day I went without easing your pain was a day I caused more of it."

Colleen focused on one step at a time, descending closer to the man she'd once agreed to marry after a week, and never regretted that decision, not even when he abandoned her at the moment of truth. She wanted to run back in her room and slam the door, a stubborn but powerful defense, but instinct propelled her forward. "*Months* you let me die inside. You seemed fine, and I was..."

Noah found his strength and rushed to assist her down the stairs. His face was visible with relief when she let him support her. "I should have thanked you, and instead, I abandoned you. If I have to spend the rest of my life making it up to you, I'll never complain about that for even a second, Colleen." He dropped his eyes. "And you're wrong. I was never fine. Not ever."

"You really hurt me." Said aloud, the words were freeing. Colleen released them so they could no longer bind her.

"I know."

"I trusted you, Noah."

Tears pooled in his eyes. "I was so, so wrong. I let my pride take over my better judgment. I don't care about the magic. It doesn't matter."

Irish Colleen and Kellan Jameson backed away to give the couple privacy.

"It does matter," Colleen insisted, straightening up with pride. "My abilities are as much a part of me as anything. You can't pick and choose which parts of me you want, and don't. That's what got us into this mess, don't you understand? It's all, or it's nothing."

Noah knelt in front of her when they reached the bottom step.

He couldn't stop the tears. "Then teach me. I want to spend the rest of my life learning everything about you, especially the things I made you feel like you needed to hide." He reached into the box he'd set aside when he came to escort her. "It's Christmas, Colleen. Marry me."

"And when you find something else about me that scares you?"

"Never." Noah choked up, shaking his head. "Never. I know what a world without you is like now, and I don't want any part of it. I swear on Skye." He extended a tentative hand toward her abdomen. She helped him, pressing it against her twitching belly. "On us."

"Her name is Amelia," Colleen answered, her voice heady with emotion. "After my grandmother. I never met her, but Ophelia said she was strong, and in this family, this is what we do. We honor our ancestors."

"Amelia," Noah whispered. "Amelia is a beautiful name."

"You can name the next one," Colleen said, reaching down to clasp his hands in hers.

"We can. Together," Noah replied, staring up at her with a joy that outweighed any fears that still remained in her heart.

Colleen's mother and sisters decorated the study, including the tall tree, with wreaths and bows of heather. They'd planned this, all of them, and Colleen had the impulse to be angry at their assumption she'd agree to the marriage, but they'd known her heart better than she knew it herself, because there was nothing in the world she wanted more than to be Mrs. Noah Jameson.

In the absence of her father, Charles gave her away. He beamed with pride as he eased her down the stairs to her waiting groom. Augustus presided over the ceremony, having secured the proper licensing after the call with Noah, where the other man spelled out his intentions and begged assistance. Kellan brought his own Catholic priest, to bless the union.

Irish Colleen, Evangeline, Maureen, and Elizabeth glowed in their purple gowns. The only one missing was Madeline.

"In the end is our beginning," Noah vowed, slipping the ring he'd had made from the old dried heather, dipped in rose gold, over her finger. "The end of closed minds and hearts. The end of hiding, of being anyone but ourselves, ever again."

Colleen tearfully repeated the words as Kellan handed her his own ring to give to Noah.

"You're family now," Augustus said, announcing their unification. "Glory and all. Scars and all." He looked directly at Noah as he said, "In marriage, you are as much a Deschanel as any of us. You have much to learn, and many willing to teach you."

When the wedding party scattered to begin the Christmas celebrations, Noah whispered to his new wife, "If you have scars, they're mine as well."

"Let's go back to Skye. In the summer," she rejoined, resting her face against the warmth of his chest. Elizabeth offered her a vision of their future, a gift Colleen knew she wouldn't give unless there was happiness, but she refused. The real gift would be experiencing it. "I think I need to be where the magic is. Ours and the kind the land offers."

You knew, she would say to Evangeline later, before returning to Scotland. *You knew and said nothing.* Evangeline, in return, would only grin and shrug.

Noah kissed the top of his bride's head. "Merry Christmas, my love."

WITH BREAKFAST EATEN AND THE GIFTS CLEARED, Augustus retired to the study to be alone with his thoughts.

He'd brought a tray of Irish Colleen's cooking to Ekatherina, but the hatred burning in her eyes was enough to send his own meal lurching to the back of his throat.

Augustus had a tenuous relationship with God. It wasn't that he didn't believe in the deity, but prayer had never come easy, nor had the idea that he was simply expected to give his troubles over to a higher power. If Augustus couldn't solve his own problems, that was a mark of failure, not faith. This was why, when Maddy died, he didn't look to the heavens for his answers or his anger. He also didn't seek his penance from God, for failing her, though he suspected what was happening with Ekatherina now was a form of divine justice.

Colleen found him huddled over, and he couldn't fault her for thinking he *was* praying, in that position.

"Oh, I'm sorry." She aimed herself back to the door. "I can come back."

"Not at all. Come in." He rolled his shoulders back and settled properly in the chair. "Who's all still here?"

"Evangeline, Noah, Kellan, Lizzy, Connor. Charles, of course. Cordelia disappeared before the wrapping paper was even cleaned up, and Maureen and Edouard left with Olivia not long after. They have a dinner planned with his family."

"So, most everyone."

"Lizzy and Connor retired to her room, and are doing God knows what." Colleen laughed. "Evangeline is napping. Noah and Kellan went for a walk along the levee. So, yes and no. If you're worried about privacy, I think you'll be good in here a while longer."

He nodded.

"Any word on Ekatherina?"

He shook his head and cast his eyes toward the silver tray where Charles kept his best booze at the ready. How many times had he talked himself out of pouring a glass? He loathed the stuff; the burn, the taste. But if he could tolerate it long enough, the sweet escape would be worth it.

"You okay?"

"Yeah, fine," he said. "Just lost in my own head."

"I won't distract you. I just wanted to come say thank you."

He lifted his head to look at her. "For?"

"Oh, come on. I know it was you."

Augustus tried to protest but laughed instead. It felt good to laugh; to feel something other than the acute sting of failure. "I was worried you might throw something at me. I'm glad it ended well. I like Noah. I like him for you."

"You did well." Colleen perched on the side of his armchair so she could hug him. She planted a kiss on his cheek. "I love you."

Until he heard the words from her, Augustus didn't realize how seldom they used them in this family. "I love you, too. Be happy, Colleen. You deserve it."

"I am happy." She rolled her hand over her belly. "In a few months, this family will have four in the newest generation. Four, Aggie. A year ago, it was just the six of us."

"The world is changing."

"We've changed, too."

He looped his hand around her waist and squeezed. "We have. But I don't remember what life was like before."

"Before?"

"Before it all changed. Maddy. Everything."

Colleen started to disagree, but she changed her words as she was saying them. "You know? I don't really, either. I can't decide if that's good, or bad."

"I don't have much use for the past, but history repeats itself when forgotten."

"Deep!"

"But no less true." Augustus smiled and nudged her off the chair. "Go entertain your husband before Evangeline or Lizzy get ahold of him."

"Husband. I like the sound of that."

Colleen wasn't gone two minutes before a series of frantic footsteps sounded on the staircase. They drew closer, and Augustus knew, even before they stopped outside the double parlor doors, that they were for him.

His eyes traveled to the grandfather clock. It was past ten in the evening. Almost the twenty-sixth, just as predicted.

He jumped to his feet as the doctor burst through.

"Sorry for the intrusion, but she's close."

Augustus followed him, wordless, forcing his mind to go blank as he ascended one step after another and made his way down the hall toward the inevitability of fatherhood.

IRISH COLLEEN CAUGHT HER ELDEST DAUGHTER AS Colleen carried a mug of tea from the kitchen. She called her name.

"Mama," Colleen replied. "Merry Christmas."

"I'm happy for you, my dearest. Noah. Amelia. This is all I ever wanted for you."

Colleen couldn't recall this much tenderness from her mother in many years, perhaps as far back as when she was too little to tend to herself. It didn't matter that she saw happiness as simple and neatly tied as marriage and children. That, if Colleen had chosen to go through life without either, her mother would stress over that decision, seeing her as unmoored.

It didn't matter, because today was the happiest day of Colleen's life, and she had no room for the bane of overanalyzing.

"Thank you, Mama." Colleen set her mug on the counter and embraced her mother. "I'm happy. Everything is as it should be."

"God provides when we most need Him."

"I believe He provides most when we provide for ourselves."

Irish Colleen reached up and patted her cheek. "That very well may be, dearest. I think it's lovely you want to honor August's mother. I never knew her, either, you know. She died very young, but he loved her so. He admired her, and he came from a time where women weren't always revered for their strength."

"He always said that she was the greatest woman he'd ever known."

"I believe he meant it. There's a special bond between mothers and sons. And daughters and fathers. You picked a good father for your children, Colleen. A good man. An *Irishman.*"

Colleen sighed internally in relief. Why had she ever worried that her mother would quibble over the Jameson name? Why did she ever worry about half the things that troubled her?

"He is," Colleen agreed, smiling. "And what you said, about fathers and daughters, it's true. I want to help Kellan reunite with his. The way he helped Noah and me find our way back to one another."

"Just be careful, Leena. I spoke with Kellan last night, when we met to help plan this wedding, and we talked about this very thing. He loves his daughters, but time is fickle. For some, it heals. For others, it severs."

"But isn't it better late than never? And what about Noah? He has three sisters he's never even met."

Irish Colleen's smile broke through her concern. "Never mind all that. You have your own family to worry about, dearest. My Colleen *Jameson*." She pressed her hand to her mouth and then lowered it to Colleen's belly. "*A stór*."

"That's beautiful. What does it mean?" Colleen had never heard her mother speak Gaelic directly to them; only to her friends. She often wondered why she never bothered to teach them, only to later realize that her mother looked back upon her years before she married August Deschanel with a degree of embarrassment. More, that she worried her children would see this time in her life this way, and be aghast to be connected with such humble, working class beginnings.

With a swell of shame, Colleen understood that they'd helped shape this belief by never asking.

Now that Colleen was approaching having children of her own, she would find the time to ask her mother these things. To learn where she came from and carry these stories down the line. It wasn't only their Deschanel heritage that mattered.

"It means 'my treasure,'" Irish Colleen answered, after a pause. "A common thing for mothers to say to their babies."

"Me? Or Amelia?"

Irish Colleen craned up to kiss her daughter's cheek. "Both."

. . .

Christmas changed Colleen's life forever, but her marriage was only the beginning. When she fell asleep just after eleven, her dreams decided the remainder of her fate.

Anasofiya Aleksandrovna Vasilyeva Deschanel was born several minutes past midnight, in the wee hours of December twenty-sixth. She announced her birth with a blood-curdling scream that matched the tenor of her mother's, who refused to hold her newborn and demanded they take the demonkin from her sight before she smothered it with her pillow.

Augustus stayed his tears as he held his precious daughter in his arms. The nurses cleaned her up, but her face bore the remains of a hard entrance into the world. He hoped her days thereafter would be only easier, but the wails of hatred coming from the birthing suite bore no such promise.

"Ana, huh? I thought—"

"I know what you thought," he said to Evangeline, when she had her turn in the quiet room with Augustus and the baby. "I don't want people to look at her and think of the tragedy of Maddy's life. Anasofiya will be her own woman someday. I don't want her living in the shadows of another."

"You still named her for a dead woman."

"I named her for my wife's sister, who never had a chance to live. And for her father. And for the world she left behind." *And I did this because it might be the one chance I have to change her heart and show her that her daughter is worthy of her love.*

"Why isn't she with her now?"

"If Ekatherina doesn't want to be a mother, that's her choice. If I think about it too much... I'll... I'll say things to her I'll regret," Augustus said, his voice hard. "But God as my witness, Evangeline, Ana will know nothing but love. Anyone who wants to be near my daughter will come to her with joy, and nothing else. She's my life now and my priority. Nothing or no one else will ever come before her."

"I like this side of you," Evangeline replied and clapped him on the back, grinning.

"Yeah?" He rocked Anasofiya in his arms, lulled by the magic of her soft sounds.

Evangeline peeled back the blanket and tickled the side of Anasofiya's cheek. "She looks like you."

He laughed. "She doesn't look like *anyone* yet."

"I meant that scowl." She frowned, taking a closer look. "Yep, that's all Augustus."

"Stop," he said, but he was playing. Happy. There was another, darker matter to attend to in the room next door, but his worries dissolved into joy as soon as the nurse transferred his daughter to his arms. He was utterly and completely in love. Not love like the healing spell of Carolina. Not love like the enchantment of Ekatherina.

Real, unfiltered, untempered, true love.

I will give you everything and will keep you safe in a way I couldn't do for your mother, Ana. You're the best part of me, and I'll make a world for you where only the light shines through.

THE PHONE RANG JUST BEFORE MIDNIGHT. COLLEEN willed it to go unanswered. She shivered under the blankets, consumed by the terror of confirmation. If no one answered, then it wasn't real. Her heart spoke a truth the rest of her couldn't accept, and she begged it to *shut up, shut up, shut up*. It wasn't possible. It just wasn't. Not on her wedding day. Not on Christmas.

Irish Colleen knocked, entering before anyone answered. Her face was streaked in red, and it looked as if she was on the verge of crying. "Colleen... I have terrible news."

"No," Colleen cried. "Don't say it." Noah stirred, but didn't wake.

"Something tells me you already know."

"I had the most terrible dream," she managed, through her tears. "She came to me."

. . .

They were lost in the garden. Colleen used to misplace herself often as a little girl, and then it became a game, because whenever Ophelia came looking for her, there was always tea and cookies after, long beyond the point when Ophelia knew what Colleen was up to.

Rich flora painted the landscape, blinding her. No, it was more than the flora, it was the light itself, as if someone had turned the contrast up to a hundred and bathed the world in extremes.

A beautiful redheaded woman stepped from behind a palmetto tree, wearing a berry-picking hat tied at her neck. It draped over her shoulders, doing her no good on this excessively sunny day.

Who are you, Colleen started to ask, but she knew Ophelia, even this version of her, the same way she would know her grandmother, or anyone else who lived in her heart.

I wasn't sure you'd come, said this younger, vibrant version of Ophelia. Oh, what a vision of loveliness she was, her cheeks bathed in freckles, lips full and red, like the begonias growing just beyond.

I always come when you need me, Colleen said, but a part of her knew this wasn't true, or perhaps feared it was not. For Colleen, abandonment was a cross she bore whether anyone else suffered from her absence or not. Her leaving Ophelia for Scotland was a sin she wasn't prepared to answer for, but she knew this was why she was summoned here now, or part of it.

I have always needed you, the young Ophelia confirmed. Always, Colleen. Always, even when you needed me more. When others look to you for counsel, you must find your comfort somewhere, and in you, I saw the future. When you are dying, the future is everything.

But you're not dying! Look at you!

This is me in my mind, at a time where I was happy... in love, but that's not your story, or why we are here.

Why are we here?

You know, my darling.

I don't, Colleen insisted, like a petulant child, unwilling to play this game anymore, because it was no longer fun. She didn't care about the tea or cookies. She wanted to go home. To wake and remember Christmas through the eyes of a blushing newlywed.

It's time, Colleen.

No. No! You have to fight it!

Yes. Ophelia laughed, a delightful sound that echoed across the flowers. You place so much faith in me, to think I can cheat death! He comes for us all, child, at some time. I have lived nearly ninety-eight years and I daresay I've gotten away with far more than I deserved.

This isn't funny. It's not the least bit funny. You can't leave me! I need you!

You've never needed me as much as you believe, my darling dearest. I've never told you anything you didn't already know, somewhere within you. If I am to be credited for anything, it's helping guide you to a place where you no longer needed me to show you.

That's not true! It just isn't. You're the only one in the world—

Hush, Colleen. The time is upon us, and I'm trying very hard to remember how this goes, because it was only described to me, and many years ago, at that. You might remember that I was the one who renewed the Council for the Louisiana Deschanels. I didn't have the privilege of having the mantle passed to me in the dream state.

Are we dreaming? Colleen could cry with relief. If this were a dream, she could wake up! She could wake up, and—

Be present! This is as real as anything, Colleen Amelia, and if you don't focus, I'll depart this earth before you have a chance to accept my gift.

Your gift? Colleen asked, but she knew.

Say the vows with me now, child. Quickly.

I don't remember them.

You? Psh. You forget nothing. God help your husband.

I don't... I can't...

In power, obligation, Colleen.

Colleen barely got the words out, but she said them.

In obligation, commitment.

In obligation. Colleen paused to catch her breath. Commitment.

In commitment, solidarity.

In commitment, solidarity.

In solidarity, enlightenment, they said together, and then, the vows of the Council, governance through enlightenment.

There is one more, that is only for you. Only for the magistrate, Ophelia said. Are you ready?

I will never be ready.

I ask you again.

I'm not ready. I am ready. I am, but—

For as the strong shall rise again, so shall the strong be governed.

Colleen hesitated before repeating. She didn't know these words, and she didn't understand them.

You do understand. You understand all too well, my darling. Our family is doomed to fall and doomed to rise, and only the magistrate can know how to govern in such chaos. The head and the heart.

What if I fail?

Say the words?

What if—

I'm fading, child. Say them. Now!

For the... for the strong... shall rise again and so shall the strong be governed.

The young Ophelia approached, and as she did, parts of her began to disappear. First the hat, then, inch by inch, her hair. Her hands dissolved into dust, and then her legs.

Her face was the last to go. It remained long enough to say her final words.

I love you, Colleen. As my own. More than my own. Now, go, and do as you are born to do, so that I can die with the peace of possibility.

I love—

But Ophelia was gone.

CHARLES FOUND AUGUSTUS IN THE QUIET ROOM WITH Anasofiya. He'd slept there, holding her, and Charles understood, because even a moment away from Nicolas was a moment too long.

This was just one more thing the brothers would find they had in common, and Charles felt a surge of closeness to Augustus that was welcome.

He brought his son to meet his new cousin. They wouldn't remember this first meeting, but it was the beginning of a relationship that would follow the rest of their lives, if he had any say in it. He'd nurture this friendship the way August Deschanel and Colin Sullivan Sr. had nurtured the one between their oldest sons.

"Did you hear the news?"

Augustus nodded solemnly. "God rest her soul. Tante Ophelia was an incredible woman, and the family won't be the same without her. How's Colleen?"

"About what you'd expect," Charles said with a heavy sigh. "These scrolls arrived not long after the phone calls, announcing the news, and Colleen's promotion to magistrate."

"Scrolls?"

"What did you expect from a council of witches?"

Augustus half-laughed. "Right. Poor Colleen. Is she ready for this?"

"Are we ever ready for any of the shit life throws at us?"

Augustus looked down at his daughter. "I suppose not. But she'll need us, all the same."

"We're the men in this family. We'll rise to the occasion, same as we always do."

Anasofiya yawned, waking. Augustus adjusted her in his arms. "Wanna hold her?"

"Let's trade." Charles handed Nicolas over and accepted the cooing Anasofiya into his arms. She was beautiful, a beauty he'd seen only in his own son, and he'd never felt closer to his brother than he did right then, not even moments before when he'd entered the room filled with brotherly love.

"This is love," Charles said. "This, right here."

"It is, isn't it?" Augustus agreed. He brushed his fingers across Nicolas' cheeks.

"These two, they have to look after each other, Augustus."

"Of course they will. They're family."

He met his brother's eyes, forcing contact. "No, I mean it. Their mothers failed them both, and we can only give them so much. They'll need each other. I wish... I wish Dad had prepared you and me better. Maybe things would be different."

"Their mothers might yet change, Huck."

"Do you really believe that?"

Augustus looked away.

"Cordelia is dead to me. Ekatherina... she's your wife, and I won't say a bad word about her, but Ana's been on this earth for twenty-six hours and still hasn't met her mother."

"The labor was hard on her. They had to bring in blood for a transfusion, Charles. It took almost forty hours! The doctors say she needs rest—"

"Stop," Charles commanded. "Stop it, Augustus. I don't know how you decide when fantasy is better than reality, but reality is what we have. And reality is, we have two babies with fathers who would *die* for them, and mothers who wished they were never fucking born." He swallowed. "Years from now, I want you to remember, your wife *chose* not to let your healer sisters fix what's wrong with her. She's choosing pain, to avoid choosing motherhood."

"You may be right," Augustus said after a long, uncomfortable silence. "But right now, all I can think about is Ana and shielding her from all of it. The rest is noise, and I don't have time for it. Not anymore."

"You're a good man," Charles said. "Better than me."

"You're a better man than you think."

"I just had an affair with my best friend's wife. Still think that?"

Augustus smirked. "I knew about the affair. I also know you're the one who ended it."

"How the hell did you know that?"

"Lizzy."

"Damn her little deviant mind." Charles rocked his new niece in his arms. Ana. Nicolas. Augustus would realize soon that he was right. These two would need each other, in a way their other cousins would never require. Their births were a nuisance to the mothers who bore them, and that had a way of marking a child. "Colin keeps telling me his marriage is broken over things he doesn't understand. For his sake, I hope he never does."

"His marriage is broken in spite of you, not because of you. Correlation is not causation."

"Come again?"

Nicolas gripped Augustus' fingers with a peal of giggles. Augustus smiled down at him in equal delight.

"Catherine's choice to be unhappy was there long before you met her," Augustus said, making faces at his nephew. "And the Charles I know would have kept going until the whole thing exploded in both your faces. You made a hard choice. I know now how tough it is to put aside what's in your heart for what you know is right."

"Sounds like you're paying me a compliment."

"Your hearing might be off, but it's possible."

The brothers both grinned as they held the babies.

"Promise me. About Ana and Nic."

"Of course. I promise."

"They may not have their mothers, but they have each other. And us."

"They won't want for anything."

"Ever."

Charles rose. "I should go. Colleen is expected at The Gardens and I don't think she's in any shape to drive herself. And if I know her, she won't want Noah anywhere near this just yet." He traded babies with his brother. "Call me if anyone else has a baby, or something."

Augustus shook his head. "Three is enough for now, I think."

"Four, shortly," Charles said. "And if Mama doesn't put a stop to that bullshit going on in Lizzy's room, we'll be welcoming baby number five soon enough."

"Hey," Augustus called, as Charles was exiting. "You *are* a good man, you know. Not the best." They both laughed. "But a good one. Dad would be proud."

Charles' eyes burned, as the missed opportunities to talk to his father dug themselves further into the past, with Maureen's ghosts now also a bygone hope.

He would do anything in the world to hear the words from August himself. He'd spent so long being the antithesis of his father that he never considered how good it would feel to be compared to him, and for that comparison to feel possible.

Disappointment was a useless emotion, though, especially now, when the whole world awaited in Lisette's beckoning arms.

CHAPTER 20

In My Time of Dying

A dark chill nipped the air of the somber Council chambers. Pierce, Pansy, and the others wore drawn, haggard faces, permeated by sleepiness from being woken to news that changed all their lives. No one in the family, present or otherwise, was from a time before Ophelia, and each of them quietly processed what life now would be like without her.

Colleen started with the vows, though she wasn't feeling any of the words. Words were just words, but they meant something when Ophelia said them. Ophelia had revived this ancient process for the family and turned it into a powerful binding agent at a time when the family was content to live disparately; to dwindle into obscurity, having forgotten where they'd come from. Who they were.

"And enlightenment through governance," Colleen finished and low voices repeated the words, sounding exactly as she felt.

"I don't get it," Pansy cried. She dabbed at her eyes, but her handkerchief was already soaked, and no longer doing her a bit of good. "I just saw her. She was..."

"Pansy, darling," Pierce ventured. His hand twitched, but it stayed put. "We've known the truth for a while. Even if we weren't ready to accept it."

"No, Daddy," Kitty replied. She hung her head low, bedecked in lace mourning garb so fine that Ophelia would have chastised her for trying too hard. "She's always been old. I thought she'd be old forever."

Eugenia and Cassius exchanged looks, but didn't offer their platitudes. Like their half-brother, Pierce, they seemed to know that to say something was worse than saying nothing, when their pain was so far beyond their control.

"I didn't ask for this," Colleen told them. She needed them to understand she hadn't strong-armed herself into this precarious role, even if deep in her heart of hearts she'd always desired it. But no internal desire was strong enough to sway the stalwart mind of Ophelia Deschanel.

"We know, dear," Eugenia said. "That's not how this works."

"I thought it would be you," Colleen said.

Eugenia smiled sadly. "Maybe once, you thought that. You've known for a while what she intended. I think we all did."

"What's done is done," Cassius rejoined. "We can lament, or move on. All in favor of moving on?"

"That's Colleen's job now, calling us to vote," Pierce said and had to look away to cover a fresh batch of tears.

"I don't have much to say. I'm sorry, I'm just still in shock," Colleen said. Her eyes fell over the row of darkened portraits, their ancestors either gazing down in love or judgment. Maybe both. She'd seen them all watching them for years, but now they were watching *her,* and she'd never felt more supported, and yet more alone.

"We all are," Eugenia said, so pleasantly that Colleen began to feel guilty for taking a role she always believed was meant for her older cousin. "And you most of all, I imagine. You were her darling, Colleen." She shook her head. "And on your wedding day. I wish I were offering my congratulations under better circumstances."

"Yeah, congrats, cousin," Pansy said, sniffling, and her sister offered the same words.

"I can't think about that right now," Colleen said. "We have so much to do."

"Nothing that can't wait until we've laid her to rest," said Cassius.

"Oh, God." Colleen sighed. She buried her face in her hands. It was all so much, so terribly much, thinking of her beloved aunt shoved into the family tomb with the piles of familial bones. "We have to coordinate that, too. I'll... I'll do that first thing, when the funeral home opens."

"It's fine, dear. The Sullivans will handle this, as they handle everything."

"For lawyers, they sure seem to possess a broad set of skills," Kitty remarked. She blew her nose into a lace doily, and then screwed her face up when the remnants ended up all over her black satin gloves.

"It's how the estate was set up, from the early days. They're not simply our attorneys, they're our lifeline. They manage anything we need, and they're paid handsomely, in times of peace, and in times of need. So it was before, so it always shall be." Pierce's bloodshot eyes regarded both his daughters with gentle scrutiny. "It will be okay," he said, maybe more for himself, to give him the strength he needed to support them, too. "This day was always imminent, and now it's here, and that's that."

Colleen had to assume some sort of control. To say *something* to refocus their attention. Ophelia would know what to do.

Child, I wasn't born knowing every little thing, you know. Start with what you do. Build your castle upon that.

"We are six now," Colleen began, because to start where she did know meant returning to the basics. "We'll need to select a seventh."

"I suppose you'll want a Deschanel," Pansy quipped, but the venom in her words didn't make it to her heavy eyes.

"It's not my choice alone."

"It is, though," Pierce said, with a degree of firmness. "It is your choice. We must all vote, of course, but the magistrate has both nomination power and final say."

"I intend to change that. What good is a Council if only one has any real power?"

"And you can, if you want," Pierce replied. "But you're right. We need a seventh, and quickly. Do you have someone in mind?"

Colleen could scream, and might if it served her in any way. "No, Pierce, when I went to bed last night my aunt was still alive and everything was still fine."

"Our aunt," Eugenia said. "Don't feel as if you have to do this alone, Colleen." She reached across the table and laid a hand on Colleen's. "We are with you. Aren't we, brothers? Nieces?"

The rest replied with nods and soft confirmations.

"Nothing has to be decided now. We have no serious matters to vote on," Eugenia went on. "Colleen, it's your choice where we go from here, but you might consider calling this meeting to an end now, so we can all go back home and tend to our grieving families."

Colleen nodded. Her throat was swollen from crying. Nothing was right in the world, with Ophelia gone. She was the compass, guiding them. The glue, bonding them. Who was Colleen, but a third child in the heir's line, newly married, still in college, about to become a first-time mother, with more distractions than a magistrate had any business with? Who was she to lead this family?

"Colleen?"

She nodded. The grandfather clock chimed five. "We'll adjourn this meeting for now. Finding our seventh is a top priority for me, no matter what else might be going on." She rose. "I'll stop by Sullivan & Associates when they open in a few hours. If they're going to handle the final sendoff for our family's matriarch, there are some details they'll need to get right."

They waited to see if she was finished speaking before they, too, stood. Even in their grief, there was an order, a way of things, and everyone in the room clung to this tradition as a lifeline through the chaos of loss.

Ekatherina died in the early hours of December twenty-eighth. Her doctor, only the evening before, had said that while she wasn't improving, she wasn't getting any worse, either, and he suspected he was close to being able to declare her officially out of the woods. The Deschanels were so distracted with the death of their matriarch, the birth of Anasofiya, and the fresh nuptials of Colleen that none of them had the presence of mind to press further for details. Ekatherina's illness was something all of them, even Augustus, thought was the product of her own resentment, something most had stopped trying to understand and were now simply angry.

Augustus had Anasofiya in a bassinet in his room while he dressed for Ophelia's wake. He was adjusting his tie when the sounds of harried activity down the hall caught his urgent attention. He opened the door to see machinery being wheeled by racing nurses, and the doctor blew by without a word.

Charles and Elizabeth appeared in the hallway, wearing the same shell-shocked expression. Without a word, they all bolted in the direction of the bedlam.

Augustus would never forget what he saw next, despite spending the rest of his life searching for ways to rid himself of this final image of his wife.

The doctor had climbed atop her with the electrical paddles. He was so unprepared for this moment that he was still wearing his pajamas as he first screamed at them to charge, and then, after several unsuccessful attempts that left Ekatherina flopping on the hospital bed, he threw them into the corner and began desperate chest compressions.

The three siblings were frozen in place by the shared vision.

"Doctor, we have to call it," one of the nurses said. She exchanged a look with another, who just shook her head.

"No! She was fine last night, and there's no medical reason for this!" His face fell down upon Ekatherina's

"Doctor, she was gone when we got here. She's been gone a while."

The doctor ignored her, caught in a frenzy of his ministrations.

"Her face is already starting to show the signs of rigor mortis.

Doctor, *look* at her." The nurse again turned to her peer and it was then she saw Augustus. "Oh, no. Mr. Deschanel, I—"

Fire swelled within the belly of Augustus Deschanel and it launched him forward. Charles caught him before he could fling himself on the bed, and Elizabeth joined in just as he rolled his head back and began to howl.

"Ekatherina!" Augustus screamed her name as he fell forward, held aloft only by his siblings. "*Ekatherina!*"

The doctor rocked back on his heels and bowed his head. "Time of death… God, I don't know. The coroner will need to weigh in."

"Ekatherina!" Every syllable was a dagger to his heart. If only he'd tried harder, tried better to understand the madness consuming her. This was his fault, he'd done this to her! He'd taken her contentment and tried to turn it into a life he wanted, and it had driven her mad and now, and now… "EKATHERINA! *EKATHERINA*!" He screamed so hard he felt something break within him, and his voice failed him when he tried again, only managing a hoarse, *Ekatherina, Ekatherina.*

"Brother," Charles said, holding firm to his arm. The warmth at his ear told him Charles was close. None of his other senses were doing a damn thing to help him. They'd failed him, as he failed her, and now Anasofiya would never know her mother, never know the woman Augustus had chosen to spend his life with, all because, because—

Augustus climbed the wall until he saw the ceiling and then everything went black.

It wasn't much of a honeymoon, and neither felt much like celebrating, but they needed their space, and Augustus needed his, and so Colleen and Noah booked a room at the Monteleone for the remainder of their time in New Orleans.

Colleen believed the Christmas Eve Maddy died was the most horrible thing that could ever happen to them. To even consider a worse feeling was both a disservice to their lost sister and an omen no one wanted to invite.

The birth of Anasofiya, the wedding of Noah and Colleen... these things were not enough to lift the pall that arrived first with the death of Ophelia and then, tragically, Ekatherina.

She should have pushed harder with Ekatherina! What did it matter if the woman didn't want to be healed, the alternative was death!

Consent is all we have to guide us correctly in the world of magic, Ophelia once said, and there was more wisdom in that than in anything else she'd ever said. Being a healer had responsibilities that went beyond healing. A responsibility to know when your healing wasn't welcome, and to respect that, no matter the cost.

Ekatherina died in a house with two competent healers, and there was nothing now they could do about it. Neither Colleen nor Evangeline had the power to raise the dead. No one in the family did, as far as she knew.

"I wish I could fix this for you," Noah offered, appearing behind her, as she stood at the window of their suite, surveying the skyline of the city that created her. Created them all.

"I don't know if I would've survived this week if not for you." Her hands over his were more for him, she told herself, but it wasn't true, because she meant what she said. Without him, she'd be lost, and this was one more sign that she'd never understood love before Noah. She didn't want to understand love without him.

There was no after Noah, she decided. If by some terrible twist of fate their marriage was not meant to last, she was determined to never search for it in another. She'd never find it.

"We can postpone both our programs for a while. My doctorate isn't on a timetable, and you could enroll in a summer term if you're worried about falling behind."

"I'm not."

"Good." He kissed the back of her head, his lips warm against her dark golden hair. "I didn't think you were."

"Two funerals in a week is more than my family can take. And at Christmas. *Again.*"

"It's more than they deserve," he said. "But if they're anything like you, there's a strength running through their veins that will get them through this."

Colleen leaned back into him. "You're my strength, Noah."

She saw him smile in the window's reflection. "I'm part of it."

"You don't give yourself enough credit."

"You give me too much," he countered. "But I'll do everything I can to live up to your image of me, Colleen." Noah lowered his arms, wrapping them around her swollen belly. "We'll make all of this work. I promise you. Amelia, your responsibilities with the Council. School. Supporting your family."

"I can almost believe it when you say it."

He laced his hands through hers, protecting their daughter together. "I want to learn everything about your world, because it's our daughter's world, too."

"Slowly," she said, letting her eyes close for a moment. Sometimes peace could be found by simply blocking out the world. "If you promise to keep an open mind."

"I promise."

Colleen spun in his arms and looked up at him. "What you said before, about postponing things. I don't want to. At least not any longer than we have to. We can leave after Amelia arrives. I'd like her to be born in New Orleans."

"If that's what you want."

"It's what I need. Staying forever won't help them, or us. Sometimes... well, sometimes leading means taking a backseat for a while."

"Wisdom from your aunt?"

"Something like that." Colleen closed the shutter on the window and moved to the kitchen for some water. "I'll fly back quarterly for Council meetings. It won't impact school if I schedule them around mandatory breaks."

"I'll come with you."

"I'd like that." She took a long sip. "There's a short trip we need to make, before we return to Scotland. Sooner rather than later."

"Where?"

"Boston," she answered, finishing off her water before dropping the glass in the sink. "To see Rory and Carolina. Huck's got himself into a world of trouble, and I think I can help him." She looked up, directly at Noah. "He can't ever know, though."

"Okay," Noah answered. "Boston it is."

"I know you don't think much of my brother..."

Noah shook his head and moved closer to her, drawing her into his arms. "He's my brother too, now, and if he's in trouble, then we do what's right and we help him."

WHITE. THE COLOR OF HIS NIGHTMARES. THE SHEET, arcing softly through the air before landing on the corpse of his wife.

He hardly recognized the man who'd flung himself at her body in consuming grief. He heard his screaming voice and didn't know who had done that. He couldn't connect with the Augustus from that day, because that Augustus was gone now, and in its place was the empty void where the light should be. Instead, there was only numbness.

Only Ana kept him moving.

She was his reason for waking. For dressing. For trying to choke down a meal, cooked by his deeply concerned mother. For listening, as the Sullivans explained what they'd laid out for Ekatherina's service. For choosing the dress she'd be entombed in.

When he was with Ana, he could almost forget both the beauty and the horror of his short, tragic marriage.

Charles, Evangeline, and Elizabeth took their turns at his side. He didn't need them, and he told them as much, but it wasn't a deterrent. Maureen also came by, passing Olivia off to Lisette before sitting silently at his side. The silence he appreciated. In the silence, one could choose, because nothing was chosen for them.

"This, too, shall pass, son," Irish Colleen said to him, but there was no value in saying things like this, because of course this would pass. All things did. The belief and knowledge in that eventual passing did nothing to allay the grief shrouding the moment. It did nothing to allay the guilt, that Augustus' grief was more for the idea of a life he wished to live than for the loss of his wife.

Only in her death could he see how wrong he'd been to marry her.

He no longer felt responsible for what happened. He was wiser than the weaknesses some men were prone to when up against the edge of their emotional capacity. This didn't exonerate him, it only clarified his role in the matter.

He'd loved her. She'd loved another. He'd failed to understand the extent of her mental illness, and in turn, she'd failed him. They'd failed separately, and together, but the one good thing they'd ever done together now lay in the bassinet at his feet.

Augustus rocked Anasofiya. She didn't sleep well, and the doctor suggested this might be because she'd never been nursed from her own mother. The wet nurse often left frustrated, returning with milk she'd expressed at home when Ana wouldn't take to her nipple. Augustus didn't know if there was any merit to the doctor's declaration, but neither did he know if his relief in Ekatherina's failure to nurse—his fear, too, that some of her darkness would transfer to Ana—was any more or less rational.

Anasofiya was his life now. He didn't know or care if there was another woman out there waiting, because to even travel that path was to put upon his shoulders an expectation that to love and be loved was all there was to live for. He had that now, in a way he could never have with a romantic love. In her few days on earth, Ana had shown Augustus what love meant. In that love, he found the darkest fear of his life.

He would try and preserve the memory of Ekatherina's happy days for their daughter, but he knew he would never fully shake the worry that Anasofiya had the darkness within her, too. If it took everything in him, so be it, but he *would* protect her from that. From herself. From her mother's nature, which made up half of her.

The wet nurse arrived. She quietly knelt by the cradle, reaching for Anasofiya.

"No," Augustus snapped. He hadn't intended to sound so harsh, but he wasn't prepared to apologize for it, either. "I'll feed her."

"But, sir, she has to learn to properly latch—"

"I said no," he repeated. "I'm all she has now, and I need to learn to do this. There's still enough milk in the fridge?"

"Well, yes, but—"

"Bring more when you can," he said, reaching to take his daughter into his arms. His only real, true love. His reason for living. "In the meantime, please hand me the bottle in the chiller and see yourself out."

Epilogue: Irish Colleen and the Seven

Colleen Deschanel, known as Irish Colleen to her family and friends, walked past the faces of her seven children, as she did every night of her life.

She could hardly bear to look at them now. This year was the culmination of her failures as a parent, a sin compounded by her helplessness to save any of them. From others. From themselves.

Charles, a new father in a loveless marriage that would never mend itself.

Augustus, a widower with a daughter he'd never ask for help raising.

Colleen, finally in love, finally married, a mother soon herself, everything Irish Colleen ever wanted for her. So why had God delivered a tragedy on her most joyous day?

Evangeline, her sweet, damaged darling, her consummate student with the hardened heart.

Maureen, in a marriage perhaps worse than the one engineered for her oldest brother, lost to motherhood in a way Irish Colleen feared was not healthy for mother or child.

And Lizzy... ah, sweet Lizzy. She'd check in on her baby soon. Her only treasure still home, but not for long.

Irish Colleen would add a new row of pictures. Her grandbabies. The fresh blood and air that would resuscitate this struggling family and breathe new life into a world crumbling around them.

She climbed the stairs, clutching her back, which burned in agony. Hardly forty, she thought, and already falling apart. As she dragged herself along, she wondered at her decision to continue this tradition with Elizabeth, who had outgrown being tucked in long before Irish Colleen was ready for her to be. Maybe one day, her grandbabies would stay here, and she could revive the ritual again with them, restoring a sense of purpose that only came from helping her little ones close out their day feeling loved. No one told her how hard it would be to raise seven children, but ah, no one ever told her how much harder it was to watch them leave the nest.

Soft, suspicious noises floated from inside Elizabeth's room. Irish Colleen ran her hands over her apron, scandalized but not surprised. She'd known what the tradeoff would be, when she called Connor home to do what she couldn't do: save Elizabeth from herself. Irish Colleen crossed herself, even though she no longer really believed that some of the things she'd been raised to believe were sins were so bad, after all. Would God prefer Lizzy in pain, or in love? Would He judge her more for what she did now, at her age, unmarried, or would He prefer to greet her early when the world He created, so lovingly, failed her?

Irish Colleen refused to believe in a God who would sooner take her baby than allow her to find absolution. This same God had given Lizzy her terrible gifts. Was it so wrong for her to find a way to live with them? Was that not what free will was about, accepting God's graciousness and creating a life worth living?

No, she'd known what would happen when she invited Connor to live with them. She didn't like it, but so much of her life had been a series of disappointments that it was easier to adjust her expectations now.

Just last night, Elizabeth confided in her that she'd seen Ekatherina's death before Augustus even married her. Elizabeth then spent months pretending to save the woman for her brother's sake, knowing every step of the way that nothing she did would do any good. That wasn't from God. If it was, Irish Colleen's faith was shaken.

Elizabeth had grown up too fast, but she'd done so in the arms of someone who loved her wholly, and for that, Irish Colleen was eternally grateful. It stung, that Connor had replaced her, but a girl like Lizzy could've ended up with someone who encouraged her demons instead of teaching her ways to live with them. Connor was an angel, sent from heaven, and nothing, nothing could ever convince her otherwise.

Irish Colleen pressed a kiss to her hand and laid it on the door. She stepped past her youngest daughter's room, palms pressed into the curve of her aching back, and went to see about readying herself for bed.

The Family

Deschanel Family (Line of August)

The Deschanel (*pronounced Day-shah-nell*) family are the line of heirs of the great Charles Deschanel of France, who settled the Deschanel dynasty in Louisiana in 1844. All current day descendants of this original Charles are either of the line of August or Blanche. Deschanels are of the line of August, and all others (Fontenots, Broussards, Guidrys, etc.) come from Blanche. August, with his wife "Irish" Colleen Brady, had seven children: Charles, Augustus, Colleen, Madeline, Evangeline, Maureen, and Elizabeth. Madeline, their fourth child, tragically passed in an automobile accident on Christmas morning, 1970.

Irish Colleen was August's second wife. His first, Eliza, he married for love, but she was unable to bear children and eventually passed away from cancer.

The rights of inheritance of the Deschanels follow the tradition of the eldest son, so Charles, son of August, is the current heir.

August (1905-1961) & "Irish" Colleen Brady (1932-)

Charles b. 1950 (m. Cordelia Hendrickson b. 1951)
Nicolas b. 1975

Augustus b. 1951 (m. Ekatherina Vasilyeva b. 1950)
Anasofiya b. 1975

Colleen b. 1952 (m. Noah Jameson b. 1950)

Madeline 1953-1970

Evangeline b. 1954

Maureen b. 1956 (m. Edouard Blanchard b. 1935)
Olivia b. 1975

Elizabeth b. 1959

Deschanel-Broussard Family (Line of Blanche)

The Deschanel-Broussard family (*pronounced Brew-sard*), are cousins of the Deschanel family, equal in wealth and prestige. Where the Deschanels are descendants of the line of August, the Broussards are descendants of the line of Blanche. Claudius Broussard is Blanche's third husband, and the children from this union are considered her most favored. She also has a son by her second husband, Johnson Guidry, but her relationship with Pierce is fractured.

Blanche did not have children by her first husband, Ellis Kenner. Both Ellis Kenner and Johnson Guidry died of "mysterious circumstances."

Blanche Deschanel (b. 1906) & Johnson Guidry (1890-1930)
Pierce b. 1926

& Claudius Broussard (b. 1900)

Eugenia b. 1940
Pierce b. 1926
Cassius b. 1942
Wyatt (1943-1955)
Noble (1944-1955)

Guidry Family (Line of Blanche)

The Guidry family are those descended from Pierce Guidry, first son of Blanche Deschanel-Broussard. Although the first son is the heir on the Deschanel side, Blanche does not recognize Pierce as her heir. Instead, she sees her second child and eldest daughter, Eugenia Fontenot, as her heir. Pierce represents his line of the family as one of the seven Deschanel Magi Collective Council. His two daughters, Pansy and Kitty, are also on the Council.

Of Pierce's children, only Pansy, so far, is married.

The Guidrys, for no reason other than Blanche's disdain for her second husband, Johnson, are considered the black sheep of the clan.

Pierce Guidry (b. 1926) & Winnifred Babin (b. 1926)

Pansy b. 1949
Alton b. 1950
Kitty b. 1954

Pansy b. 1949 m. Placide Lafont b. 1945
Rex b. 1973

Fontenot Family (Line of Blanche)

The Fontenot family are those descended from Eugenia Broussard-Fontenot, second daughter of Blanche Deschanel-Broussard. Although Eugenia is a second child, and a daughter to boot, Blanche recognizes Eugenia as her heir. Eugenia is married to Wallace Fontenot, and they have three sons. Eugenia represents her line of the family as one of the seven Deschanel Magi Collective Council.

The Fontenots are well-respected in the community, with a similar prestige as their Deschanel cousins.

Eugenia Broussard (b. 1940) & Wallace Fontenot (b. 1939)

Luther b. 1962
Llewellyn b. 1963
Lowell b. 1964

Broussard Family (Line of Blanche)

The Broussard family are those descended from Cassius, third child and second son of Blanche Deschanel-Broussard. Cassius is married to Helene Barrow, and they have two children, a son and a daughter. Cassius represents his line of the family as one of the seven Deschanel Magi Collective Council.

The Broussards, like the Fontenots, are well-respected in the community, with a similar prestige as their Deschanel cousins.

Cassius Broussard (b. 1942) & Helene Barrow (b. 1944)

Jasper b. 1963
Imogen b. 1965

Sullivan Family

The Sullivans are one of the oldest and most trusted families in New Orleans. A family of attorneys, a majority of Sullivans, most notably males until recently, join the family law firm, Sullivan & Associates, which has been a New Orleans staple since 1839. The family came up through the ranks, by their bootstraps, with humble beginnings as Irish immigrant laborers. The Sullivans are both the attorneys and friends of the Deschanel Family. Like the Deschanels, the designation of heir follows the eldest son, and so Colin Sullivan Sr. is considered the head of the family. His father, Patrick, still lives, but in quiet retirement.

Colin Sullivan Sr. (b. 1932) & Josephine Bartleby (b. 1931)

Colin Jr. b. 1950 (m. Catherine Connelly b. 1948)
Rory b. 1952 (m. Carolina Percy b. 1953)
Patrick b. 1953
Chelsea b. 1956

Sullivan & Associates

Sullivan & Associates is a family-owned law firm, and one of the oldest and most trusted in New Orleans, founded in 1839 by Aidan Sullivan. Comprised mostly of Sullivans, the firm is considered something of a birthright for any Sullivans looking to go into law. They have represented the Deschanel interests for over a century. Charles Deschanel's best friend, Colin Sullivan Jr., as well as Colin's two brothers, Rory and Patrick, all plan to join the family firm one day. Colin Sullivan Sr. is the current Senior Partner, following the retirement of his father, Patrick. Colin Sr. and his brothers, Jerome and Jamie, are the figureheads of the firm.

Homes & Properties

Oak Haven

The old Victorian mansion Irish Colleen and seven used to live in, on Chestnut and Sixth in the Garden District, just beyond Lafayette Cemetery No. 1. Although there are larger (Magnolia Grace) and more storied (Ophélie) homes in the family possession, August Deschanel chose this particular property to raise his family in with the thought of giving them a more "normal" upbringing than he had.

The Gardens

The colossal mansion and family seat of the Deschanels at Jackson Ave., taking up an entire square block between Coliseum and Prytania in the Garden District. The Gardens also houses the cavernous chambers where the Deschanel Magi Collective and the Collective Council meet to discuss family business. The architectural style of the estate is Italianate, and the most notable feature is the extensive, exotic garden wrapping around the property, shielding the home from outside view. Ophelia Deschanel occupied this house for many years, as the long-standing Magistrate.

This house is now Colleen's, as the next Magistrate of the Deschanel Magi Collective.

Ophélie

A large plantation and surrounding lands purchased by Charles Deschanel I, built in 1844, and currently occupied intermittently by the Deschanel family. Charles will inherit the property as the heir to the estate. Located near Vacherie, an hour west of New Orleans, the Greek Revival ivory mansion on the Mississippi River is secluded from the road by gates and foliage. The estate has forty-five rooms and large ornate gardens, as well as two hundred outbuildings from when the property was a working plantation. Charles, as the heir, has inherited this property.

Magnolia Grace

A beautiful, traditional Greek Revival mansion in the Garden District that once belonged to Fitz Deschanel (the second son of Charles I), and has ever since been passed down through the second sons. Augustus Deschanel inherited this property, which is located on Prytania, near Eighth.

Deschanel Media Group

The brainchild of Augustus Deschanel, who had dreamed of starting his own company since he was a young boy. The company's vision is a magazine for locals, which both catered to the elites but also offered an opportunity for aspiring writers to get their short stories published and in front of potential patrons.

Femme Forte

A sprawling Northshore mansion along Lake Pontchartrain, considered the birthright of Blanche and her descendants. The property will be inherited by Eugenia Fontenot, her favorite child.

Blanchard House

An old, esteemed mansion along St. Charles Avenue in the Garden

District, passed down through the Blanchard family over many generations. Though an exceptional home, Edouard keeps it dark and in some degree of disrepair.

Weatherly Estate

The vast, columned Uptown home of Daniel Weatherly Sr., gifted for his patronage of Tulane. His son, Dan Jr., is a good friend of Charles Deschanel. The estate is located near the sister universities of Tulane and Loyola, by the Ursuline's Academy.

Also by Sarah M. Cradit

KINGDOM OF THE WHITE SEA

Kingdom of the White Sea Trilogy

The Kingless Crown

The Broken Realm

The Hidden Kingdom

The Book of All Things

Blackwood Cycle

The Raven and the Rush

The Poison and the Paladin

Southerlands Cycle

The Sylvan and the Sand

The Flame and the Forsaken

Guardians Cycle

The Altruist and the Assassin

The Belle and the Blackbird

Darkwood Cycle

The Melody and the Master

The Hand and the Heart

Sceptre Cycle

The Claw and the Crowned

The Duke and the Disciple

THE SAGA OF CRIMSON & CLOVER

The House of Crimson and Clover Series

The Storm and the Darkness

Shattered

The Illusions of Eventide

Bound

Midnight Dynasty

Asunder

Empire of Shadows

Myths of Midwinter

The Hinterland Veil

The Secrets Amongst the Cypress

Within the Garden of Twilight

House of Dusk, House of Dawn

Midnight Dynasty Series

A Tempest of Discovery

A Storm of Revelations

A Torrent of Deceit

The Seven Series

Nineteen Seventy

Nineteen Seventy-Two

Nineteen Seventy-Three

Nineteen Seventy-Four

Nineteen Seventy-Five

Nineteen Seventy-Six

Nineteen Eighty

Vampires of the Merovingi Series

The Island

and more

The Dusk Trilogy

St. Charles at Dusk: The Story of Oz and Adrienne

Flourish: The Story of Anne Fontaine

Banshee: The Story of Giselle Deschanel

Crimson & Clover Stories

Available as a single collection, The Shorts

Surrender: The Story of Oz and Ana

Shame: The Story of Jonathan St. Andrews

Fire & Ice: The Story of Remy & Fleur

Dark Blessing: The Landry Triplets

Pandora's Box: The Story of Jasper & Pandora

The Menagerie: Oriana's Den of Iniquities

A Band of Heather: The Story of Colleen and Noah

The Ephemeral: The Story of Autumn & Gabriel

Bayou's Edge: The Landry Triplets

For more information, and exciting bonus material, visit www. sarahmcradit.com

About the Author

Sarah is the USA Today and International Bestselling Author of over forty contemporary and epic fantasy stories, and the creator of the Kingdom of the White Sea and Saga of Crimson & Clover universes.

Born a geek, Sarah spends her time crafting rich and multilayered worlds, obsessing over history, playing her retribution paladin (and sometimes destruction warlock), and settling provocative Tolkien debates, such as why the Great Eagles are not Gandalf's personal taxi service. Passionate about travel, she's been to over twenty countries collecting sparks of inspiration, and is always planning her next adventure.

Sarah and her husband live in a beautiful corner of SE Pennsylvania with their three tiny benevolent pug dictators.

www.sarahmcradit.com

www.ingramcontent.com/pod-product-compliance
Lightning Source LLC
Chambersburg PA
CBHW020334310726
48979CB00015B/2366/J
9781958744284